The Soul Power Series

Dragonsoul

To Shannon,

Thanks for all the walks and hanging out over the last several years.

Phoebe Nabors

Phoebe Nabors

Phoebe Nabors

Copyright by Phoebe Nabors 2017

First printing, 2018

ISBN 9781976386824

Chapter 1

Conner woke from a disturbing dream and looked around his unfamiliar room, taking in every detail of his surroundings to distract himself from the uncomfortable experience. A small desk sat in the corner of the room with his sack and a single candle on top. Next to the desk was a chamber pot he'd never used, and a window stood just above it, revealing a clear sky and the beginnings of a beautiful sunrise. Other than the desk, there was really not much in Conner's small room: a wooden stool he had carved himself, a small cabinet for an extra change of clothes, and a rarely used bed.

As he sat up in bed, he thought of how odd it would appear to an outsider that he didn't have much in this chamber to show that it was occupied, but what the outsiders didn't realize was that he didn't stay often enough in this one-room apartment above his Dictator's house to really have a need to make it feel like home. It was, after all, his least favorite of his many homes.

Conner was a traveler. He was not a traveler like so many others, who had something to sell or just wanted to explore. No, Conner had a purpose, a purpose he sometimes resented and almost always kept hidden. Few people knew what he was, and that was by design. It wasn't that he wasn't honored, or even proud that his Dictator had chosen him, but he would have also liked to have had a choice.

He pulled on his brown cotton shirt and loosely tucked it into his trousers. Grabbing his sack from the desk, he exited his room and headed downstairs to grab a piece of bread before meeting Byron for a hunt. Conner had long ago learned that if he didn't acknowledge his Dictator, Philimina, he would let him leave without a word, but even a stray glance in his direction was perceived to be an invitation to discuss as much time as had passed since their last meeting. It had been thirty years since his last visit.

As Conner slipped out the door of Philimina's house, he surveyed the street for potential danger; an old habit he had never felt the need to break. Seeing nothing of concern, he walked to the small stable next to the house and untied the lone horse. He knew Byron would sense how bothered he was and he would have to tell him about his dream, but he couldn't help but hope that just once Byron would be distracted by other things.

It did not take long to reach the city gate as Shiloh was a small town with only the one street running through the middle of about a dozen buildings. Several larger farms were scattered about the east side of the town, making up the majority of both the area and population, but Conner had rarely visited any of them, as nothing lay to the east for a good hundred miles. He would soon reach the stream just outside of Shiloh and had no idea how he would explain to Byron what he had dreamt.

Conner saw the stream appear before his eyes; its cold water always sparkled in the sun, giving it the appearance of cut glass. Years ago, when he and Philimina had been on good terms, Conner had bathed many mornings in that stream, feeling that no other water in all of Ephriat could make him so clean; surely, no other water tasted as good. As soon as he arrived at the stream, he dismounted his steed and led him to the water. After watering his horse, Conner reached for the wineskin in his sack and, dumping out the contents, sank to his knees, and plunged the wineskin into the stream, filling it with the refreshing liquid.

"Good morning, Conner." He could hear in his mind the soft hello of his oldest friend. Every time Byron spoke to him, it felt like a soft caress to his mind.

"Mornin' Byron," turning around, Conner looked straight into the emerald eyes of one of the largest dragons he had ever met. Dragons, when born, were not much larger that puppies, but they grew quickly and never fully stopped until they died. This makes judging the age of a dragon rather easy for anyone who knows them, and, though Byron could not confirm it, Conner was quite sure he was nearly seven hundred years old.

"You are not yourself this morning," Byron looked at Conner with mild concern, never missing any hint that his most precious friend was troubled.

"I had a strange dream, nothing more." Conner knew that his explanation would not fly, the very fact that he had had a dream and still remembered it upon waking was strange. With this in mind, Conner calmly told him of the dream. It had not been disturbing, in the normal sense of the word; there had been nothing disgusting or gross about it, only how real the dream had seemed disturbed him, as this meant that it was likely not a simple dream, but a vision.

As Conner began to explain, the water from the stream transformed his words into pictures until the dream became real once again and Conner was back in the meadow that had been the setting for his vision.

An old man draped in a cloak walked carefully toward Conner and spoke his name, he seemed to know Conner, though he was sure he'd never seen the man before. "There is a girl in the town of Jaboke, she is young and fair and in search of something precious."

"What does she seek?" Conner lived for moments like this, when he felt that he could help someone in need of assistance. If a young girl needed him, he would give any help he could.

"She does not seek that which she believes she does, but you must aid her in her search nonetheless." The old man did not speak a demand, but rather he spoke with the knowledge that Conner would stop at nothing to help her, whatever it was that she needed. "You will know that she is to be trusted and aided by her knowledge of your magic." Without even the smallest of an explanation, the old man quickly turned and walked out of the meadow as he came, leaving Conner alone in his strange environment.

As the last word was spoken, the water in the stream smoothed again, trickling over the rocks on the bed of the stream as Byron looked calmly at Conner, assessing the wisdom of following the old man's advice. Visions rarely gave any clarity, so the vague speech of the man's instructions was no surprise, but they could not be sure if the thing this girl sought was anything they should help her acquire. However, that they must help her was the one thing he had stated unequivocally.

Knowing that they could not ignore a vision such as this, Conner and Byron rose from their place beside the stream and went in search of Byron's four younger brothers: Dagmar, Grezald, Grizwald, and Snarf, the youngest.

It did not take long to find the four large dragons playing in a nearby field. It never ceased to amaze Conner how different one town was from another; in and around Shiloh, dragons and magic users were welcome, but in Jaboke, Conner would have to find this mysterious girl alone because dragons were feared and magicians were not welcome. Even though technically, Conner would not be welcome either, no one asked visitors if they had magic, and if anybody asked if he was a magician, he could honestly tell them that he was not. He was so much more than a magician that it was insulting that they were foolish enough to lump all magic users into that one category.

At seeing the pair approach, the four younger dragons ceased their play and turned to Conner and their brother. Dagmar was the second oldest and had the most unusual coat Conner had ever seen; all dragons are covered in closely packed scales, with the softest fur imaginable growing in the millimeters of space between each scale, but most dragons Conner had seen were all one color, even if they had hundreds of shades of that color on their enormous bodies. Dagmar, however, was mostly blue with white areas on the underside of his wings. This coloring helped him blend in well with the sky as he flew. Grezald and Grizwald were identical both in their size and in their dull orange coat and dark green eyes; Snarf was the smallest and least ferocious looking dragon Conner had ever seen with his royal purple fur and gentle gold eyes.

"Conner has had a vision and we will be leaving immediately for Jaboke in response to this dream." Conner knew that that was the only explanation any of his friends needed, but he also knew that Byron would fill them in on the details silently for his sake.

The journey to Jaboke took several days because Conner insisted on bringing his horse, which, they had learned years ago, would not be carried by any dragon. The journey was not unpleasant, though, because of the constant conversation between brothers. Even though Conner was not a true part of their family, they had claimed him as their brother when he was only a young man.

Some days, it seemed only a few years ago that he had been introduced to the group by a young girl whom he had befriended not two miles from their hunting grounds, but other days he felt every one of his three hundred plus years. He had one of the most powerful Dictators that ever lived, so he had always expected to live a very long life by human standards, but his life would still be over long before any of his dragon brothers. Having seen what losing Lorahlie, Byron's mate until she had been murdered several years ago, did, not only to her mate but also to the other dragons, Conner was determined to find a way to prolong his life even further, if only to save them the pain of losing another loved family member.

Having arrived at the outskirts of Jaboke, Conner and his brothers settled for the night, though the sun had not yet sunk beyond the horizon. "You have all been suspiciously quiet these last few hours," Conner looked toward Snarf, who was apparently laughing at something spoken only among dragons. "Please, tell me you aren't planning on attacking the poor town for their fear of dragons."

"That does sound appealing," Dagmar spoke and let out a slightly cruel laugh, *"but that isn't what we were discussing in the least."* Dagmar looked to his brothers and laughed in earnest. Snarf had apparently told a joke that he didn't want Conner to be privy to.

"Conner," Snarf apparently thought it time to include him in the discussion, *"do you remember how Lorahlie would periodically give you a complete makeover?"*

Conner remembered immediately, Lorahlie had always said that Conner would blend in better as a young man because he walked with too much confidence to be so old. She had used magic to keep his teeth healthy and straight, erase, not only gray hair, but even wrinkles, and occasionally she would do something drastic like changing the color of his skin completely. Conner had never minded the "up-keep" as she had called it but had seen no need to bother with trivial things such as aging since her death. "Yes, I remember. What about that had you all laughing so much?"

As soon as he'd asked the question, he wished he hadn't. Snarf had a mischievous look in his eyes that could only mean one thing. "No!" Conner held up his hands to show them his seriousness, "I will not allow you to use any kind of magic on me. Lorahlie was one thing, but I do not trust you enough."

"Aw, come on Conner," Snarf purred in his most logical voice possible, *"This poor young girl is gonna get one look at you and run the other direction. You*

don't want to scare off the very person we're supposed to be helping. Do you?"

Seeing the others nodding in agreement, Conner knew that he had been beaten. He supposed did not mind so much, after all, it would feel good to be repaired again. "I will not trust myself to a prankster such as you, Snarf," he at least had to minimize the damage this young dragon might be planning, "If I'm to be repaired, I want Byron to do it." With that, he sealed his fate. Even Byron, in all his seriousness, would enjoy the amusement of transforming Conner into a new person.

As Byron began to throw around ideas for improvement, Grizwald produced a mirror for Conner, reminding him that Lorahlie had always had him look at himself before a transformation. The old man in the mirror did not look much like Conner felt, he was about six feet tall and had obviously been a muscular warrior as a younger man, but his hair was almost white and his skin was wrinkled and sagging. He looked to be about seventy years old, not bad considering his true age, but quite unattractive in any event. Conner found it odd that he could feel so young and strong and look so old and frail, but that was the nature of what he was.

As Conner stood staring at his reflection, he became surrounded by a white aura. It had been a long time since he'd been in his true form, as he saw no need to show off his dragon-like wings and sharp eyes, and since any one of his brothers would gladly give him a ride anywhere he needed to go, he also had no need for them. But in his true form as a Dragonsoul, he was more easily formed with magic, and so any time he needed to alter his appearance, he would transform into an enormous creature standing over seven feet tall, with huge, silky, black wings.

Soon, the magic was all finished and the dragons were admiring their work. Conner looked again at his reflection and smiled. He was almost six inches taller than a minute ago, and his hair had returned to the inky blackness of his youth. His formerly wrinkled skin had been stretched and smoothed over his once again youthful body. He didn't know why he cared about his renewed youth since it was only the surface of him that had been changed; he felt no different than he had a few minutes ago. Only now, he looked as good as he felt.

"Ok, Conner, time to stop admiring yourself," Dagmar laughed gently as Grizwald made the mirror disappear as easily as he had made it appear moments earlier.

"The sun is beginning to set, and we may have a very big day tomorrow," Byron stepped in as the voice of maturity, as he always did. Soon every dragon was curled on himself and Conner was safely tucked under Byron's large wing.

Chapter 2

Aleisha hurried from the kitchen holding the largest basket she could find; she had to hurry to the market before Melvin closed his shop for the day. Exiting the mansion, she quickly surveyed the streets, scouting out the quickest path through the crowd of people bustling about, either headed to or coming from the market at the center of their small city.

As she strode down the street, skillfully weaving through the mass of bodies, she couldn't help but notice the differences between those who worked for a living and those born to wealth. Rich women wore slightly tighter dresses made of fine linen and draped with lace and dyed vibrant blues and purples, while poorer girls wore slightly looser clothes of earthen tones made of cotton or wool. Aleisha was the exception. She was a slave, but she was better dressed than some of the richest women in town, as she was owned by the richest, most exorbitant man in Jaboke. Even so, she had to take care not to bump into any of the women who belonged to a higher class than her, so she aimed for the gaps between families and young working girls.

As she headed past several stone houses toward the center of town, she saw almost a dozen knights on horseback. She assumed that they were looking for the magicians that had supposedly been seen closer to Jaboke than the city leaders would allow. The people of Jaboke were a superstitious lot, and they feared anything that they did not deem natural.

When she finally arrived at the market, she made her way toward her favorite merchant to purchase some missing ingredients for the dinner that she had been ordered to cook. She was not the regular cook, but on the evenings that her master was home in time, he liked for her to prepare the meals because he enjoyed watching her work. He would be furious if he knew that she had let some of the more common ingredients run out. "Good morning, Melvin." Aleisha greeted her good friend as she entered his shop.

"Good morning Aleisha, what can I get for you today?" Melvin turned to Aleisha when he heard her voice, instantly recognizing her. He was a stout old man with more gray in his hair than black.

"I need to get some carrots and a pound of cheddar." She thought for a moment before continuing, "Do you have any strawberries yet?"

Melvin began gathering her order into a burlap sack and turned toward her again, "Not yet Aleisha, sorry. I'm expecting them either the end of this week, or the beginning of next." As he weighed the cost of her purchases, a large man, about six and a half feet tall with build of a warrior, stepped into the shop.

"Good morning," Aleisha greeted the stranger, noting his short dark hair, wise eyes, and gentle expression. Somehow his eyes looked familiar, but she wasn't quite sure why.

"Mornin' miss." The stranger smiled as he greeted her.

"My name is Aleisha, are you new to our town?" She tried not to stare at the man, but there was just something about him that she couldn't quite figure out.

13

"Conner," he smiled again, "Yes I'm just passing through. I just stopped in to see if anybody would give me directions; I can't seem to find the stables."

"They are on the east side of town." Her father! His eyes reminded her of her father's eyes. Even though her father's eyes were bluish green and radiated cold like a winter night, and this man's eyes were dark and kind, there was something undeniably similar about them. They both looked like they had seen and done things most people couldn't even imagine. They held a confidence and a wisdom that most men could never have. "I doubt that they'll let you in, though; magicians are not allowed."

He cocked his head in confusion, his smile from a moment ago disappearing, "Magician?" he looked offended by the accusation.

Could she have been wrong in her assumption? Maybe he had gained that expression from a life on the road? No, she had met many travelers, and none held the calm yet powerful expression that she had only ever seen in her father and now this man. Her father had been a magician, and the guards were looking for a magician in Jaboke. "Yes, that is what I said, magicians are not welcome in Jaboke."

"What makes you say I'm a magician?"

"Your eyes," Melvin was trying to look like he wasn't listening to their conversation, but she could see him sneaking a look at them as he wrapped her things. "You hold the expression of a man who has seen and done things that I can't even name."

14

He smiled again, looking a little relieved, "That's because I travel with dragons. I can assure you that I am not a magician."

Dragons? She supposed that made sense and instantly felt horrible for her accusation, and if this man had access to dragons, she certainly didn't want to upset him. "I am so sorry, I suppose I shouldn't have assumed."

"That's quite alright, it was an understandable mistake." His gentle smile convinced her that he was sincere.

"So, how many dragons do you travel with?" if she could get on his good side, this man could be her way out of Jaboke.

"I travel with five on a regular basis," she was surprised he answered so freely, but he looked pleased she had asked. Maybe he would be just as pleased to show his friends off in this small city.

Aleisha stepped closer and whispered quietly, "Have you ever heard of the Elixir of Life?"

"Yes," he replied cautiously, clearly surprised by the inquiry, "I have been looking for it for quite a few years now."

"I can get a detailed map to the elixir drawn by my mother, who was the last person to have used it. If you and your dragons get me out of here, I'll lead you to it." She knew it was foolish to trust this stranger, but she would do anything to get away from her master, Cedrick.

Conner hesitated a moment before offering her a half smile, "We could do that."

Conner headed straight back to the outskirts of Jaboke, where he had left his brothers, knowing that they would be eager to hear that he had found the girl so quickly and just as eager himself to get back into the town to begin their journey. At the gate, one of the guards that he had seen earlier stopped him and asked if he had witnessed any magic use within the town's walls, telling him to report if he saw anyone acting suspiciously.

Almost immediately after exiting Jaboke, Conner saw either Grezald or Grizwald flying in the distance and, apparently seeing Conner, dive toward the ground. Conner had expected them to watch for him, but he would have thought that Dagmar would have been the eyes in the air, being that he blended in with the sky so well. Conner mounted his horse and urged him into a quick gallop, even more eager now to tell them about the plan that he had made with Aleisha.

As Conner neared the dragons, he slowed his mount down to a trot, allowing it to rest before the mad dash they would be making through the town later that day. *"Back so soon?"* it had apparently been Grezald in the air as he was the one who spoke now. *"Did you already find the girl?"*

"Her name is Aleisha, and she seeks the Elixir of Life." Conner was satisfied with the looks his brothers gave him; they were perhaps more eager to find the elixir for Conner's sake than he was. "She is a slave of one of the rich men of the town, so will need us to steal her from him before we can begin our journey." Conner quickly told them of the plan before they all settled into a comfortable silence, each one too nervous and exited to speak. Snarf had eagerly volunteered to do the physical kidnapping of the young slave, a job that Conner had expected to go to either Byron, as leader, or Dagmar, who seemed to enjoy playing the villain any time foolish townspeople expected it from a dragon.

"Do you trust this girl, Conner?" Byron spoke to him then, breaking the silence that had apparently stretched too long.

"I see no reason not to," Conner spoke to Byron through his thoughts; he rarely did this, as the whole group was usually involved in the conversation, but the way Byron said his name told him that the others could not hear him, and Conner did not want to disturb the others with one side of a conversation. *"I was sent to find her by a vision. If the Lord bothered to send a messenger to tell me to aid her, I cannot see distrusting her until she gives me reason."*

The sun had moved far enough across the sky at that point that Conner estimated that it was about dinner time for Aleisha's master. This was the time for them to begin their assault on the town. Conner mounted his horse once again and wished he could explain the mission to it as he could to the others; he did not necessarily want to be on a horse, even this horse, when it was being chased by five dragons, as this one was about to be.

The group quickly arrived at the town, Conner leading on his horse and the dragons remaining hidden amongst a few of the buildings just outside the town until Conner entered through the gate. The moment the horse's back foot entered Jaboke, Conner heard the roar of one of his brothers right above him. His horse ran. Conner was flying through the town at dangerous speeds as five dragons flew after him, four of them darting between

17

buildings and trying to draw as much attention to themselves as possible, as if they needed to try. Dagmar even dove at a few pedestrians, changing directions just as the poor fools were convinced that they'd breathed their last. Snarf broke off from the group almost immediately, moving toward the large mansion that Aleisha had pointed out earlier that day. It did not take long for the chaos in the streets to attract the attention of the guards, and, before too long, several of them began throwing spears at the dragons that had undoubtedly come to terrorize their town. It never even occurred to them as they beckoned for Conner to hide behind their protection that if four dragons wanted the town destroyed, that it would already be aflame. They were so blinded by fear that they could not think rationally enough to realize that, even if they did hit them, mere spears would do absolutely no damage to adult dragons.

Aleisha had just finished making the dinner her master had ordered and was headed to his quarters to clean up the mess from the night before when she heard the commotion from the street below. Conner and his dragons had arrived as quickly as she had expected them to, but now she hoped that they would move slowly enough for her to find the map that Cedrick had stolen.

In his room now, Aleisha moved toward Cedrick's desk by the balcony window and removed the desk key, which she had slipped from the pocket of his cloak as she hung it up from dinner, from her hidden pocket. As she neared his desk, she almost choked on the stale smell of his expensive mead. Cedrick was quite fond of alcohol and spent many nights passed out drunk from over-indulgence. She found this habit repulsive, but it often provided the household with some much-needed peace when he succumbed to the strong drink. She slid the key into the lock in the top drawer of Cedrick's desk and turned it carefully, slowly, to ensure it made no sound. Inside, she found her mother's map, as well as more than a few letters that appeared to be progress reports on Cedrick's own search for the elixir. Aleisha smiled to herself at the thought of all the frustration the enchanted map must have caused her master; he didn't realize that only she could read it.

As she slipped the map into her pocket, Aleisha heard a scream from the street. This one was much closer than the last had been, indicating that it was time to make her way to the balcony. As she turned to head toward freedom, though, she paused. Did she really want to leave this? It was true that she was a slave, but she was Cedrick's favorite slave, and because of this was better dressed, better fed, and better educated than most of the other women in Jaboke, slave or free. Did she really want to leave the safety of Cedrick's mansion with a man she didn't know and five magical creatures that could kill her without a thought? Yes, she wanted to be free. She had to be free, and no fear of the unknown would stop her from chasing that freedom, even if she died in the foolish pursuit.

At her master's horrified cry, Aleisha dashed to the balcony, slowing only enough to grab a potato sack that she had stuffed her few possessions in. The moment she reached the balcony, she saw a dragon flying toward her with incredible grace and speed. Even the great eagle that made its home near Jaboke could not compare to its beauty.

"Aleisha!" she let out a frustrated growl as she heard Cedrick's voice behind her. He could not stop her now. Not when she was so close to freedom. "Move! Can't you see the dragon coming?" Aleisha turned slowly from the balcony, making a show of how she had been watching the panicked townspeople, and not the sky.

"Master," she may have overplayed her confusion a bit, "I'm sorry, sir, but I thought you said 'dragon'." She was glad that her burlap sack looked just like a sack of potatoes, so she only appeared to have stopped by the balcony on her way to the kitchen to see what all the commotion was about.

She saw his expression suddenly turn to one of panic an instant before she felt a quick jerk, and then she was flying above the streets. The force of the sudden change almost made her lose her grip on the sack, and she had to fight to breathe as her lungs were crushed under the pressure of the huge talons. When she looked up, she saw only a deep purple underbelly and two large wings. She had never seen a dragon before, much less one so close. The large creature had almost metallic looking scales covering its entire body with silky fur growing between each scale, giving the beast the appearance both of hard armor and soft fur, depending on how the light caught it. The creature was magical just to look at; she couldn't imagine what it would be to see it fight.

The dragon flew her out of town as arrows and spears flew their way. They took a different route than Conner and the other four dragons, flying north as the others slowly made their way south. Aleisha quite enjoyed seeing the town she had spent so much of her life in from such an unfamiliar perspective. As they flew, Aleisha noted the field that she had grown up tending until Cedrick decided he would enjoy her rare beauty in his own home where he could better show off his most treasured possession to his wealthy guests.

They reached the Desert Mountains long before Conner and the other four dragons. When they finally arrived, Conner seemed to be deep in a one-sided argument. "I told you that you would have to be patient," he paused for a moment before continuing, "No, you had to look wild." When he noticed her watching him, he stopped talking and glared at the largest dragon. After several minutes of watching his expression change drastically and often, Aleisha saw Conner turn to her. "Aleisha, these are my friends," he pointed toward the largest dragon, the one with whom he had just had the stare down, "This is Byron, the oldest," Byron was a deep red with emerald eyes; he spread his wings proudly and revealed their silkiness before bowing his large head to the ground. "This is Dagmar," he pointed to a light blue dragon with white splotches under his wings; he looked like he would blend in with the sky if he flew high enough. His eyes were pure white, almost like snow. He stood on his hind legs to show off his size; he was almost as large as Byron. "Calm down Dagmar, you've hardly even met her." Conner glared at him before moving on to a dull orange dragon with green eyes, "This is Grezald," he pointed to another dragon with identical coloring and size, "and this is Grizwald."

"How can you tell them apart?" Aleisha turned away from them in wonder.

"It's simple really," Conner responded with a half-smile, "if you mess up their names, they'll yell at you." He winked at Grizwald, "They're twins."

"Of course," Aleisha turned to the remaining dragon, the purple dragon that had flown her out of Jaboke was smaller than the rest. "Who is this?"

"He didn't tell you?" Conner directed a shocked expression at the smaller dragon. "What were you two doing while waiting for us?"

"Just waiting," Aleisha stared at Conner and his dragon as they exchanged looks.

"I'll let him introduce himself." He walked to Byron and sat down.

"Wait, can dragons talk?" she called after him.

"Not Exactly," She jumped as she felt, more than heard, a new voice not belonging to either her or Conner. The voice didn't seem to originate from anywhere specific; it felt like a new idea or a sweet memory that hadn't been there a moment earlier. *"We can communicate, but only telepathically. My name is Snarf."*

As he said it, Aleisha felt a powerful surge move through her; something about his name was inexplicably majestic. She stared at him for a moment, struck dumb by the powerful experience. "So, when Conner glared at you, you were conversing?"

"Of course," Snarf repositioned himself and lowered his enormous head to her much smaller one. The movement would have been menacing in other circumstances, but Snarf seemed nothing but gentle.

22

"Fortunately, only who I want to hear my thoughts can."

"So then, is he hearing this?"

"Only your side," Snarf raised his head and appeared to be thinking, *"I am very impressed that he trusts you; he doesn't even allow his Dictator to speak with us anymore."*

"His dictator?" where was this man from? She couldn't think of a single nation currently being ruled by a dictator. She turned toward Conner and saw him glaring at Snarf with a look of shocked annoyance. "How far have you traveled?"

"Oh, no," Snarf shook his head, *"I wasn't referring to that kind of dictator, I simply meant…"*

"That's enough chatter for now." Conner interrupted their conversation with one final glare at the large dragon. "We should make preparations for tomorrow," he nodded to her burlap sack, "Is that all you brought?" He seemed able to switch between hard and frustrated and kind and gentle at will.

"It's everything I own," two dresses, a comb, and a ribbon to tie her hair back was more than most slaves had, just another advantage to being Cedrick's favorite.

"I will gladly carry it." She heard Snarf's voice in her head again and momentarily wondered how long it would take to get used to the sensation.

"Oh, no I can…" Aleisha stopped when Conner gave her a strange look.

"You are not a slave anymore, Aleisha," she heard no condemnation or correction in his voice, "allow him to treat you like a lady." She nodded. She wasn't sure how else to respond. No one had ever treated her like a lady.

Conner offered her a small smile before turning to Byron, pausing for a moment, and nodding before turning back to her. "Night will fall soon, we will rest here and in the morning we will head out." He began to turn away and added, "We won't be needing to fly tomorrow, will we?"

"No," Aleisha pulled the map from her pocket; suddenly remembering that she had never even looked at it, "We won't be needing to fly for a while." She hoped she could figure out how to read her mother's map, but on the few occasions that she had glimpsed one of Cedrick's maps, it had looked to her like a relic from another world.

"How exactly are you planning on keeping Aleisha warm?" She found it odd that Snarf felt it necessary to allow her to hear his question. Conner turned around then, looking apologetic.

"She can sleep with Snarf," he looked suddenly angry when he said it, speaking between clenched teeth. Snarf must have added something that he hadn't allowed her to hear.

Seeming totally unfazed by Conner's mood swing, Snarf lay down and summoned Aleisha to him. She approached cautiously, apprehensive at the idea of sleeping next to such a powerful creature. Seeing her concern, Snarf spoke again, *"Don't worry, you'll be perfectly safe with me."*

"What if you have a dream?" Aleisha was pleased that she sounded far less terrified than she felt.

"Dragons do not move when we sleep." He said it so matter-of-factly that Aleisha said no more and curled up next to him. Snarf draped his wing over her, covering

24

her entire body and sealing in warm air that she would be grateful for when the desert air became too frigid to bear.

The dragon's warm fur was softer than she could have imagined and was so comfortable that she fell asleep almost immediately, though she hadn't been aware that she was tired.

Chapter 3

When Aleisha woke up, she saw Conner and his horse, but no dragons. Conner was sitting by a fire, cooking something that smelled delicious, but foreign. "Mornin'," he offered a cheerful greeting when he saw that she was awake. Aleisha decided that she liked his smile better than the scowl he seemed to enjoy wearing just as much.

"Good morning," she mumbled as she got up and headed toward him; she'd always hated mornings, and resented the fact that she had always had to get up early to wait on Cedrick. That this man apparently enjoyed mornings bothered her slightly. "What are you cooking?" She sat down beside him and huddled closer to the fire. The sun wasn't up yet and the desert was always freezing until then. That was one of the reasons that, even though it was so close to the town, people from Jaboke rarely ventured into its extreme climate.

Conner smiled again, "Lizard. Snarf dropped it by for you; they all left earlier to go hunting. If they can get enough to eat today, then they won't have to go again for a few weeks." Aleisha nodded sleepily, not really listening to whatever it was that he was saying as he continued to gab endlessly. "Snarf thought that you would want it fully cooked, though," Suddenly, she wished that she had been listening. What had she missed? He tried to hand her a large piece of meat that she could never eat on her own.

"How much do you think I eat?" she chuckled as she grabbed the hot meat and tried not to picture Snarf, such a gentle creature, killing it.

"What's wrong?" Aleisha looked at him quizzically, and he continued, "You're looking at it like it's still alive."

"Just tell me that it wasn't cute." She didn't know why, but the idea of eating this once-living creature disturbed her more than it ever had before; probably because she was still half asleep. When Conner did not answer her immediately, she looked up and saw him shaking violently and covering his face; trying not to laugh at her, no doubt.

"Snarf will be offended if you don't eat his kill," he said, finally looking at her, amusement still dancing in his eyes as he struggled to regain a serious expression. "At least try to eat it." She had never had a problem eating dead creatures before and didn't see why this should be any different, so she concurred. As her teeth sank into the food, her mouth exploded with the amazing flavor of the tender meat. Letting out an involuntary sigh, she chewed contentedly on her breakfast.

"So, how long do you suppose they will be gone?" Aleisha had eaten about half of her food when she found it was too much to finish.

"They could be gone for most of the day." Taking her remaining meat, Conner stood up and strolled toward his horse, the sun had come up, and he was obviously ready to leave. After wrapping the lizard in a cloth and placing it in his sack, Conner mounted his horse. "They will catch up with us, but we do need to go. This desert is not a good place to be hanging around all day," he held a hand out to her, indicating that he expected her to join him.

"I can't ride a horse," Aleisha started walking ahead of him and his steed and pulled the map from her pocket. Her mother had had a magician put a spell on the scroll when she was born, making it so that only Aleisha could read it. Unfortunately, as she stared at the unfamiliar shapes and lines on the map, she was reminded that she had no idea how to read even an ordinary map, much less a map with a spell on it. Did she have to do something to the map to make it work, or was she just supposed to read it like any other map? It would be helpful if she knew how to read any other map, but right now she was as confused as anyone it was designed to keep out.

As she stared at the parchment and hoped that she was headed in the right direction, she noticed that there was no sound coming from the horse or the man who was supposed to be following her, so she turned to see Conner staring at her with an odd expression. "You don't need to know how to ride; you only need to tell me where to go."

She bit her lip and thought about telling him her problem, deciding against it when she thought of how little she knew about him. From what she had seen thus far, she would guess that he would either grin and say that it was ok and they could figure it out together, or he would summon the dragons to roast her alive, assuming his anger didn't burn hot enough to do it himself. With that decision made, she ignored his confused expression, and began walking again for a moment before turning back toward him. "Why did you trust me so easily?" Her

sudden question seemed to take him off guard, as he
only stared at her blankly for a beat, before a slow smile
spread across his face.

"Get on the horse and I'll tell you," he reached his
hand out again. This time she took it and allowed him to
swing her up on the horse behind him. Aleisha felt
extremely out of place and awkward atop a horse; she
had never been on such a great beast as this before, and
her skirt draped over the entire back of the animal as she
attempted to straddle it like a man would and a lady
never should. Not knowing what to grab hold of, she
folded her hands neatly in her lap and adjusted her body
to keep her balance as the animal moved beneath her.
Conner seemed amused by her choice, but moved the
animal farther into the Desert of Tyree in the direction
that Aleisha had been moving. "Last week, while I was
staying in Shiloh, I had a vision. The Lord had sent a
messenger to tell me that I would find a girl whom I
would know by her knowledge of magic. He said that I
was to help her find something she sought." Conner
paused, "So, when you made that comment about me
seeing things no one else had, I thought that you were
the one I was looking for. My suspicion was confirmed
when you mentioned the Elixir." By now, the desert sun
was scorching Aleisha's back and drying her sweat
almost as quickly as her body could produce it. In that
moment, she was glad that Conner had made her get on
the horse; she couldn't imagine having to trudge through
this heat with only the occasional wind gust as relief.

"Conner," she just had to ask what had been bothering
her for several miles now, "why is it that I'm cooking
and you haven't even broken a sweat yet?" She could

see his back stiffen as she asked this and heard him mumble something under his breath just before his shirt became suddenly saturated with moisture. As much as this piqued her curiosity, she suspected that he would ignore any question she asked.

"May I ask why you weren't afraid of me?" Conner spoke, breaking the silence that had stretched for the last several minutes. "Living in Jaboke your whole life, I would have expected that you would be afraid of a man whom you assumed to be a magician."

"I don't mind." Aleisha stared at the horizon, admiring the way the blue sky stretched on for miles with never a white spot to blemish the beauty against the sparkling sand of the towering Desert Mountains. She had always loved the simple beauty of nature, so unlike man's feeble attempt to improve upon the great Maker's masterpiece, the world known to all as Elbot.

"Aleisha?" Conner brought her back to their newly revived communication attempts, reminding her that she had a question to answer.

"Oh, sorry," she refocused her attention on Conner and began, "I figured that, just like not all slave owners are as cruel as mine was, not all magicians could be as evil as the people of Jaboke would have me believe." Aleisha turned back to looking at the landscape, "I have seen the eyes of an evil magician; you don't have the same cruelty in yours. You look kinder, gentler than him." Again, she thought of the cold, harsh eyes of her father. She'd only met him once, but it had left an impression.

"I'm surprised you would have met any magicians at all in Jaboke. I thought that they never allowed magicians inside their walls; much less welcome them into the home of one of their wealthiest citizens." He had a way of asking questions that made him sound genuinely curious rather than demanding answers. Maybe this was how normal people spoke, but she really appreciated feeling like she was allowed to refuse an answer.

"My father is a magician," again, she saw his back straighten as the horse slowed to nearly a stop.

"Your father?" he sounded shocked and angry. "Your father is a magician? Why would he allow you to be sold as a slave?"

"My father is the one who sold me." She couldn't see his face, but she could tell that he was furious. "I was an unintentional consequence of his search for the Elixir of Life. I told you that my mother was the last person to have had access to the Elixir. Well, my father knew that as well and tricked her into trusting him. He lured her into his home with expensive gifts and vows of his undying affection." She wasn't sure why she felt so comfortable talking to him; she would normally never reveal so much about herself, especially to a stranger. "For years, he tried to convince her to reveal its location, saying that they would live together forever, but my mother sensed that he only wanted it for his own gain, so she refused.

"Eventually, he gave up and locked her in a cell with hopes of torturing the information out of her. When I was born, he sold me to the first man who made an offer." She stared out at the sand again, remembering Cedrick's cruel hands as he grabbed her by the arms and carried her to the cart that would take her away from her beloved mother.

31

"Greetings Aleisha, Conner." She had been so deep in her own thoughts, that she hadn't heard the thunderous beating of the five dragons' wings as they approached.

"Good morning," she tried to appear cheerful, but the seriousness of what she'd just revealed to Conner made that task difficult. "Thank you for breakfast."

Snarf landed next to them and spread his wings on the sand, *"It was my pleasure to serve you,"* he bowed his head reverently, making her laugh. She immediately felt herself relax.

"It's not my place!" Conner's sudden outburst startled both Aleisha and the horse on which they were riding. She flailed her arms, trying to regain her balance before falling off the back of the horse and crashing onto the ground with a loud thud. What was that about? He sounded angry again.

"Sorry 'bout that ma'am," he had jumped off the horse and was extending a hand to help her up. But that made no sense, wasn't he upset with her? She reached for his hand and let him pull her up before looking around at the other four dragons who had arrived back from hunting. Either Grezald or Grizwald looked quite dejected. Maybe Conner had been yelling at him rather than her, as she had assumed. "Are you alright?" he looked sheepish as he continued holding her by the arm, "I shouldn't have startled you, I'm sorry." She nodded, uncertain of the proper response. No one had ever apologized to her before.

"I'm ok, I just wasn't expecting..." she wasn't sure how to finish. She wasn't expecting what? She wasn't expecting to be thrown from the horse, she wasn't expecting him to suddenly become angry for some unknown reason, and she wasn't expecting him to show her kindness even as he remained visibly upset about something. This entire trip was unexpected to her. Servitude suddenly felt very simple; at least it was predictable.

"I should also apologize, ma'am," an unfamiliar voice echoed softly in her mind. *"It was me that upset him. I should have been more considerate."*

She looked between the repentant dragon and the man in front of her. She wasn't sure if Conner could hear the dragon's words, but she somehow felt the need for his permission to respond to him. "Grizwald wanted to apologize on his own behalf, and I could see no reason why he should not." She nodded again, still uncertain how to proceed.

"Thank you, Grizwald, for your concern," she sounded stiff and formal even to her own ears, but she was not sure how else to proceed, "I'm alright, just startled."

"We should continue." A third, deep voice entered her mind, *"You'll be more comfortable once we get a bit higher."* Higher? What did he mean by 'higher'?

"Aleisha can ride with me," Snarf spoke now, sounding quite cheerful considering the awkwardness of the last few moments. She couldn't help but smile at him; he seemed like he was always kind and upbeat. *"I'll be certain to fly carefully with her."* That's what he meant by higher. She supposed it would be cooler with the wind blowing constantly.

"I'm sure you will, Snarf," Conner smirked at the large purple dragon before turning to her, "I believe you've made a life-long friend." He turned from her then, and walked over to Byron, stepping onto his forearm in order to climb onto his neck.

"Wait," she suddenly noticed the horse in the corner of her vision, "What about your horse? Are we just going to leave him?"

"He'll follow." He didn't seem worried about it, "He always does." Conner nodded toward Snarf, who had stretched out on the ground to make mounting him easier, "You might want to climb on, I promise it's more fun riding his back than his claws."

Aleisha moved toward Snarf, uncertain and afraid of what would come next. Flight would be exhilarating, she was sure, but falling from the back of a dragon sounded much more damaging than falling from the back of a horse. *"I will never drop you, Aleisha,"* he lowered his head even farther to bring them face to face, *"I promise, you will be safe with me."* It was so easy to take him at his word. He sounded so sincere. She had always been able to tell when Cedrick was trying to trick her; the false smoothness of his voice revealed what it had been meant to hide. But this creature seemed to have no deceit in him; she didn't have to be afraid of him.

Taking a fortifying breath, she boldly approached his outstretched limb and climbed, clumsily, onto his back. Settling into the space between his shoulder blades, she grabbed hold of a handful of fur on his back and mentally prepared for flight.

Chapter 4

"Snarf?" they had been flying for several minutes when Aleisha finally spoke. "Can I speak to you silently like Conner does?"

"Someday you will be able to. Conner has been with us since he was young, so he has had a long time to learn, but it will take months for you to learn to project your thoughts to us, seeing as you are without magic." Snarf answered without hesitation. He seemed to welcome her questions where most people despised them.

"So, a magician can learn it faster?"

"All magic users can speak with dragons simply because they have magic. No learning is needed." Conner and Byron flew up next to them as Snarf spoke; Conner appeared to be listening to someone speak. Could he be hearing Snarf, or was he talking with Byron?

"She is clearly confused, then, about the nature of magic; perhaps you should explain to her." Byron's must have been the deep voice she had heard earlier. Why was he letting her hear him now? *"Ah, but that fear comes from misinformation. I suggest that we are all safer if these falsehoods are cleared up."* Byron bent his long neck to look at Dagmar before nodding towards Snarf.

"Do you realize, Aleisha, that not all humans with magic are magicians?" Snarf spoke, and then paused, waiting for an answer no doubt, but the question made

no sense. Isn't a magician a human with magic? What else could they be? *"Magicians are the most common magic users, but they are not the only ones. In fact, there are three other types of magic users, all of them much more powerful than the magicians."*

"What are magicians then?"

"Magicians are, very simply, humans with magic." Conner spoke now, his voice carrying surprisingly well in the wind, "All that makes them different from you is their ability to use very basic magic and a lengthened life. The other magical humans are Dragonsouls, Darksouls, and Lightsouls; they are all much more powerful than any mere magician and any of them would be offended to be called one." He paused and scratched the nape of his neck, clearly looking for an effective way to explain. "The reason that magicians are the only ones so many people know about is that they are the most plentiful. There are only a few hundred of the more powerful magic users at any time."

"Why?"

"There can only be as many magic users as there are Dictators." He watched her for a moment before continuing, as if gauging her reaction, "Dictators are immortal humans who have the power to bestow magical power on humans. Each Dictator chooses a baby, at birth, to wield whatever power that specific Dictator has to offer. The strength of the Dictator determines the strength of their chosen babe." Aleisha nodded in understanding, "Each Dictator can only have one chosen babe at a time and must choose a new one when theirs die. This usually results in a very close bond between Dictator and babe," Conner paused again,

36

looking remorseful, "but not always." She could feel Snarf tense beneath her weight as he said this. Byron, too, looked uncomfortable with the subject. Conner shifted his pain-filled gaze away from her and fell silent. No one seemed willing to break the silence, as everybody pointedly averted their gazes from each other.

"So," she couldn't stand the awkward silence any longer, "what is the most powerful magic user?"

"Dragons!" A husky, unfamiliar voice responded harshly. *"Dragons will always be the most powerful."* The hostility evident in the unknown voice caused her to shrink back in fear. She had forgotten her place again; she often stepped out of line when she started asking questions.

"She was clearly asking about humans, Dagmar." Snarf jumped to her defense immediately, *"No need for you to get so defensive."*

"This is a difficult question to answer, Aleisha," Byron spoke again, *"Some say that Dragonsouls are the most powerful because they are most like dragons, the original magic wielders, and are the only ones able to fly. Others say that Lightsouls are the most powerful because they can transform their bodies into that of an animal, a unique power that even dragons do not possess. Still others believe that Darksouls must have the most power because they are corrupted by it, though I will always blame the magic wielder for his wrong actions rather than blaming the magic. I am in the minority with that attitude, though."*

"An easier question to answer would be who the most evil magic wielders are." Dagmar spoke again, huffing a cloud of smoke as he finished.

"Darksouls," the disgust and pure hate in Byron's voice were evident as he hissed the answer. *"If I ever encounter another Darksoul, I will cook him where he stands."*

"And I'll help," Aleisha felt like she couldn't keep up with the constant change of atmosphere; she had not expected such a violent response from Byron, who seemed to be the calm voice of reason, or from Conner, who seemed more melancholy than passionate in his hatred.

"Surely they can't all be evil," she reasoned, but, at the glares and growls she received in response she added, "Why?"

"The Dictators of Darksouls are despicable men who are easily bribed into choosing babes who will be reared for specific purposes, like wars and politics. The lust for money that the Dictators succumb to inevitably produces corrupted men who abuse their power." Conner turned toward her again when he was finished and smiled at her, "That's enough for now; you should try to get some rest while we look for a good place to get water."

She leaned back on Snarf's back until she was laying snuggly between his shoulder blades, and pulled her mother's map out of her pocket. She would either have to figure out how to read this stupid thing, or admit her idiocy to Conner and the dragons. She would have to do it soon; she didn't want to end up in the Waves of Might, the rolling hills of southeastern Ephriat, just to discover that they should have been heading toward Gennesarat, a fertile plane on the exact opposite side of the continent.

Night fell quickly, and Aleisha was no closer to deciphering her mother's map than she had been that morning, though she had spent most of the day studying it as she rode on Snarf's back. Though she was grateful for the chance to ride on the huge dragon, she was worried that they moved much faster than the horse, and might be traveling that much faster away from their intended destination. She couldn't imagine how she would admit that she couldn't read the stupid thing, especially since at least Dagmar already didn't seem to trust her.

They had landed a few minutes ago, and Conner had wasted no time forming a pit for Grezald to spit some fire into, which he was now using to reheat the remainder of Aleisha's breakfast lizard. Meanwhile, Byron was rummaging through a few animal carcasses that they had gathered over the course of the day, it had been amazing to witness such a large creature dive so gracefully through the air and snatch up various creatures before he was ever detected. Aleisha scooted closer to the fire; it had dropped several degrees in the past ten minutes, and she was getting cold.

The desert climate amazed her. All day she had prayed for some relief from the triple digit temperatures and had been grateful for the cooler air from flying at such great heights, but even so, she had spent all day waiting impatiently for their next water break. She had been fascinated as she watched the dragons use their magic, digging a small hole into the sand before one of them would stare intently at the ground until water would slowly start to bubble up from the bottom of the hole, wetting the sand and forming a small pool from which everybody would take a drink. It amazed her that, once the water began gathering in the pool, it never seemed to run dry, no matter how much she drank.

Conner always made a point of complaining about being treated as a child each time Byron demanded that he drink, but she suspected that he craved the refreshment as much as she did. He and Byron seemed to have a very close relationship, almost like they were brothers instead of mere traveling companions.

"Deep in thought, I see." Conner spoke as he sat down next to her and handed her lizard to her.

"Yes," she hadn't intended for it to come out as a sigh, it had just happened.

"Do you need to talk about something?"

Searching for anything to talk about but the stupid map, Aleisha answered slowly, "I was wondering if," she bit into her lizard to buy some time, "Well, I was just curious about your reaction when Byron mentioned Darksouls. It seemed your hate for them is a very personal one."

For one moment, he looked slightly disappointed by her answer, but then his expression transformed into one of sadness. He turned to stare at the fire before them, as if it could give him some way to answer her. After a moment, he sighed, "There were seven of us at one point." He swallowed loudly, as if trying to choke back tears, and continued, "There were six dragons and me. Lorahlie was the sixth dragon; she was Byron's mate." The fire crackled and she, also, was now staring into it, sure that she knew what was coming, and equally sure that she didn't want to hear it. She pried her eyes away from the fire to apologize to Byron for asking, when she saw a most rare sight indeed, a sight that stopped her from saying anything more. The dragon was crying. Byron sat motionless, eyes closed, seemingly at peace if not for the tears that splashed onto the dry ground. "A Darksoul named Tallen visited the Forest of Karr on the appointed day of a certain magic user's funeral." Aleisha watched the fire again as it started to dance, forming the body of a man in a cloak riding through thick foliage. Conner's voice became a fleeting narration as the flames began to tell the story. "He was looking for a Dictator who had just had to watch his chosen babe die from a curse put on him by a Darksoul, perhaps even Tallen himself."

The lone rider had stopped right in front of one of the virtually invisible houses of the woodmen. He wore a long cloak that was signature for any Darksoul; it was dark gray at the hood, and gradually became darker as it reached the ground, ending in a black void that seemed to suck the light out of the air around it, making the edges hard to define. The hood was large and folded over his face, hiding his eyes and nose and making him impossible to recognize. "I seek Briganti." As he spoke, it became evident that he was drunk with power. That, along with his request to speak with Briganti, suggested that he was here with advice on who should replace Gabriel, whose funeral had not even yet ended.

"You're not welcome here Tallen," an old man stepped out of the shadows to address the intruder. In the colorful and bright Forest of Karr, neither man looked like they belonged; the Darksoul was intimidating and dark, and the Dictator was gloomy and dressed in black clothing, though for a less sinister reason. The woodmen slowly made their way out of the tree-like houses to watch the exchange. Among them, Conner stood with an old woman who appeared to have been crying.

"Oh, but I have come to mourn with you, Briganti. Such a sad thing to watch your faithful babe die so painful a death," the Darksoul sneered as he said it, trying to look sincere no doubt, and shifted his gaze to Conner, who looked at least twenty years older and six inches shorter than Aleisha thought he was. "I see dragon boy is here. Tell me Conner, did you cry at Gabriel's funeral, or is it true that you were born without tears?" Conner's mouth twitched into a sneer before he returned his expression to a stony indifference, "If it is true, you would make a wonderful dragon, heartless creatures that they are." Conner growled at that and barred his teeth, abandoning his effort to be civil.

"Tallen, I see that you are no wittier or wiser than the last time we met." Tallen laughed at Conner's insult, seemingly delighted to get a response out of him, and then turned back to Briganti.

"I know that you are hurting," his voice was low and sympathetic as he spoke, "not only for the loss of your chosen babe, but also for the need to choose another for great power; an overwhelming task in such a vulnerable time." He took a step closer before continuing, "My wife is pregnant and will give birth within days. You have my permission to take my baby to fill this need."

Conner and Briganti both looked toward a large clump of trees growing around each other. It looked like it could be the woodmen's version of a palace, and out of it came a beautiful dragon. This dragon had silky red fur and scales like Byron, but it was lighter and less intimidating. "Tallen, surely you know that we have many pregnant women for Briganti to choose from. Do you really think that he would give such power to a monster like you?" Her sweet voice was like velvet as she placed a gentle spell on Tallen and waited for it to take effect. After a moment, Tallen remounted his horse and rode out of their humble town without a word.

Conner got up and placed another log on the fire, though it didn't really need it yet. "Night fell and we all headed to bed," he pointed to the fire as if to tell her that the story wasn't over yet. When she looked back into the flames, she saw Byron.

"Lorahlie, your spell was made for a common person; he will be back and hungry for revenge," Byron spoke gently to his mate, lovingly admonishing her for her ill-advised intervention. She should have known not to involve herself with a Darksoul when Conner was there to handle it.

"I only made him leave peacefully; Conner would have been in a fight with him in moments if I had not stepped in. Besides, it's not as if I cursed him with leprosy. Why should he thirst for revenge?" Just then, the canopy of green leaves burst into flames.

"Why should I thirst for revenge?" the entire tree filled with thick, black smoke as Tallen spoke. "No one uses magic on me and lives to tell their children." Byron roared at the sound of Tallen's voice and moved to strike in the direction it was coming from, but the Darksoul had sent him, dazed and confused, to the Desert of Tyree, where he collapsed in pain from the poison in the smoke.

"My dear Lorahlie," Tallen's voice was as saturated with poison as the air in the canopy, "do not fear. Your dear friends will not be harmed; I only believe in punishing the guilty for their mistakes." Lorahlie coughed violently as she tried to remember which direction the door was. If she could push the fog of the poison away from her clouded mind, even just a little bit, she could fight her way out of it.

The large dragon stumbled about, trying to make her way to the exit while being choked by the wicked smoke. The pain was unbearable as the smoke coated her throat with thick tar and the poison sent an inescapable fog to her brain, causing it to send confused messages of pain to every part of her being. After just a few moments, Lorahlie collapsed, unable to continue her fight against the cursed smoke.

Conner, Snarf, Dagmar, Grezald, and Grizwald watched helplessly as Lorahlie stumbled about. Tallen had placed a barrier just outside the threshold, keeping even their voices, both silently pleading, and loudly calling, out of reach of her ears. Together, the men watched in horror, searching for a way to release her from her poisonous prison, until they heard the frantic flapping of wings above them. Byron landed seconds before his mate collapsed onto the floor of their forest home. Tallen had kept her alive just long enough to allow her mate to witness her succumb to the accursed smoke, thus completing his revenge.

As the great beast crashed to the ground, the flames calmed to their usual crackling. Aleisha stared for a moment, unable to believe what she had just heard, or seen for that matter. Since when did fire dance to show her a story? Had she just experienced magic? Had it been Byron or Snarf who had added to Conner's story? She had many questions, and chose to focus on these ones because they were not as painful as the thought of seeing such an obviously loved friend die at the hands of a wicked creature as Tallen.

"*Aleisha,*" Snarf laid on his stomach as he called for her, "*Night has fallen.*" Lifting his large wing, she could not help but think that he was offering her comfort as much as warmth.

"*Snarf,*" Snarf's wing flew up quickly, as he moved away from her like he had been burnt. He then lowered his head, staring at her in wonder.

"*You shouldn't be able to do that yet!*" the way he said it could have easily been either accusatory or admiring.

"What did I do?" Aleisha returned his confused look. She had just been under his wing, thinking of the many things she would ask him tomorrow; she had done nothing.

"*You spoke to my thoughts,*" Conner sat up and rubbed his eyes, apparently awoken by the midnight commotion. He must have been sleeping rather lightly.

"I couldn't have," Aleisha shook her head, not believing, "you said that it takes months to learn how." Aleisha's challenge was ignored as she heard Snarf now informing Conner.

Conner became thoughtful and looked toward Dagmar, who snorted and made a comment about her not being trusted. Glaring at Aleisha, he added, *"Is there something you would like to tell us, magician?"*

"I'm not a magician," Aleisha responded, just as hostile as Dagmar, who growled at her response.

"What do you think Byron? Trust her words, or her actions?"

"Both," Conner answered for Byron, "you know very well that it is possible to have magic and not know, and this is the first sign that we have seen that she is, in fact, a magic user."

"That's hardly proof that she's telling the truth." Dagmar was not giving up, *"Any magic user can hide their magic if they are careful."*

"That is absurd!" Aleisha did not know why he despised her so much, but she would not have him accusing her of lying to them. "I don't even know how magic works, much less how to use it."

"Aleisha, silence might be most beneficial right now." At least Snarf still seemed to be on her side, *"Dagmar is very good at using your words against you, and if he convinces Byron that you are a danger or that you have been lying, you will most likely be sent away."* She could believe that, not another word would be coming out of her mouth. Hopefully, the same could be said of her mind.

Minutes passed and Grizwald joined them. Aleisha was pleased that Snarf defended her to each of Dagmar's attacks and accusations, and was equally pleased to hear Grizwald join him. Conner didn't take a side, arguing any point brought up by either side. He seemed only to care that every possibility was thoroughly examined, and twice tried to convince Dagmar to take her at her word. Byron remained silent as he watched the interaction, much like a parent assessing his children's disagreement. Grezald stood by his side, staring at Aleisha as if seeing her for the first time; if he spoke, he did not allow her to hear him.

"Snarf," She tried to speak like the dragons, unsure if she was succeeding, *"can you hear me?"*

"Yes, but I do hope you aren't letting anybody else hear you; Dagmar will only be more upset by your continued use of magic."

"I think you are the only one," she glanced around the group, pleased to see that everybody else was still fixated on the argument, *"Can't you use magic somehow to see if I'm lying?"* His expression changed slightly to one of amusement. *"Sorry, it just seemed like there should be some way to know for sure."*

"Byron," Snarf spoke loudly, trying to drown out the argument, *"Why don't we check her?"* he looked back at Aleisha then, who was shivering in the cold by now, *"We have enough power in this group to force her into her true form."*

"Wait, what?" She didn't like the sound of that. "What do you mean, 'force her into her true form'?"

"Every magic user appears just like any normal human under normal circumstances," Conner seemed pleased with the suggestion, as he was now nodding in agreement, "It is obvious that you do, in fact, have magic, otherwise, you would not have been able to speak to Snarf the day after meeting a dragon for the first time. Because we know you have power, we should be able to change you into your true form, to see what kind of power you have." He reached up to scratch his neck as he looked for his next words, "You can only change into your true form if you know already what power you possess, so if we can change you, then we know you were lying and we will deal with you accordingly. If, however, we cannot change you, then we know that you were telling the truth and we cannot fault you for what you did not know."

"Will you consent to our magic?" Byron's deep, powerful voice once again filled her mind, *"It will not hurt, but you might be frightened by the trance I will have to put you in."*

"Ok," suddenly she wasn't sure if she wanted to; that warning sounded ominous. "I'll do anything to get this over with."

Byron stepped toward her and reached out a huge red paw to her, *"Give me your hand."* As soon as her fingers touched the fur of his paw, the world stilled.

Chapter 5

Aleisha stood in a wide-open field that was pulsing with white mist. She sensed a strong power in the mist and wondered if it was magical. The air all around her was still and silent, yet the mist swirled and danced as if it had a mind of its own. It slowly moved along the ground in no apparent pattern at all, until, she noticed, that it was all headed to the same location. The mist swirled around her, crawling up her arms and flowing through her hair; she could feel the magic in it seeping into her every pore, saturating her body with strength and power.

As she breathed in the intoxicating power, she could suddenly understand how one might become addicted to the sensation, but before the mist had completely soaked into her being, it exploded out away from her. The sudden flash of light she saw as the mist quickly departed from her body momentarily blinded her, and when she regained her vision, she was no longer surrounded with formless mist. All of the white power had gathered together before her and held loosely together in the form of a young dragon. As Aleisha watched the translucent being glide over the ground toward her, she saw it begin to transform again. By the time the creature stood in front of her, she was staring at a perfect image of herself, gazing back at her with an unfamiliar look in her eyes. The misty version of herself seemed to know something that was still hidden to Aleisha; her eyes seemed as full of wisdom as Conner's had the first time she met him.

With a jerk, Aleisha opened her eyes and saw five dragons and one young man staring at her. It took her a moment to recognize her traveling companions, as she was slightly dazed by what she had just seen. As she looked at each of the sets of eyes around her, she noted that most of them registered some amount of shock and wonder. Dagmar, however, looked disgusted. *"You are a very powerful magic user,"* Grizwald was the first to speak, knowing that she would want to understand what had just happened. *"You have soul power, Aleisha."* As she tried to get up, she discovered that the world was still pulsing, though the white mist was gone, and Conner stepped beside her and caught her as she almost collapsed. Whatever Byron did to her drained her of whatever energy she had left.

"The important thing is that she didn't change." She felt Snarf's wings fold around her as he spoke. She barely heard Dagmar's frustrated concession, as she drifted, finally, to sleep. She dreamt of the white mist, not understanding what it was, not knowing what it meant. She only knew that it was important, and that it was powerful.

Aleisha woke to Conner's voice; he had apparently been awake for quite some time and seemed to be talking about her. The flattery did not outweigh the annoyance. "We could teach her how to use it; she would be much easier to travel with if she could control it."

"And who do you think would have the patience to teach such a young magic user?" Byron spoke now,

apparently not caring who heard him, *"I've done that before, I would prefer never to try again."*

"Snarf could teach her, I'm sure he would be happy to," he paused then, speaking quietly when he continued, "If she's a Dragonsoul, we could welcome her; a family can never get too big."

"Now I think you're just..." Byron seemed to notice her then and nodded a greeting to her.

"Mornin'," Conner flashed his usual smile her way and ceased his conversation with Byron.

Aleisha just nodded and moved out from under Snarf's wing. She was far too tired to greet anybody, but it was too hot to remain under the furry warmth of Snarf's enormous wing. "What are you all talking about?" she mumbled.

"Your magic ability," Conner had the decency to look uncomfortable at being caught talking about her, "We were discussing the possibility of teaching you how to control it."

"Controlling it?" Aleisha looked at Snarf, "Like becoming a real magician?"

"Not quite," Byron replied, *"You have too much power to be a magician in any sense of the word,"* Aleisha remembered Conner saying something about that, about magic users with soul power being offended at the title of magician, like the term indicated a performer more than a powerful human. *"Whatever you are: Dragonsoul, Lightsoul..."* he paused for a moment and looked away from her. *"You have had this power since birth, or shortly thereafter, depending on how quickly your Dictator chose you. So, you are already a 'real' magic user."* Snarf sat quietly beside Aleisha,

watching the interaction. He seemed to be considering adding something, but looked reluctant. *"It is, of course, up to you whether or not you learn to use your power."*

Aleisha looked to Snarf, hoping he would say whatever was on his mind, *"What do you think I should do?"*

"My opinion is that, while the Dictator that gave you your power had a choice in who to give it to, it was ultimately the Creator, and not your Dictator, who gave you this power. With that in mind, I see no reason that He would give you the power if He did not intend for you to learn to use it."

"But why would the Creator give this power to a slave?" She couldn't even imagine the Creator acknowledging her existence; the idea that He would hand pick her for this power was almost laughable.

"I'm quite sure that the Creator of the universe knew when you were conceived, and even before that, that you would not always be a slave."

"You don't need to decide right now," Conner spoke from right beside her, "This must all be overwhelming for you; yesterday you were a slave, but today you are a powerful magic user. None of us would blame you if you weren't ready to fully accept this new reality."

"Speak for yourself," she heard Dagmar grumble in annoyance.

Aleisha nodded absentmindedly, trying to ignore Dagmar's constant negativity, and walked toward Snarf. She felt like the girl that she was just a few days ago was quickly disappearing, and she wasn't sure how to adjust to all the changes. It wasn't just the idea that she had magic now; if it were just a matter of possessing something she was unaware of, she felt like she could handle that. Nothing was as it had been, though, she was free now, yet she suddenly felt like servitude was not so bad. She had known who she was. She was a slave. She belonged to someone and, while she didn't like it, she knew what to expect from each day. There was a simplicity, a familiarity in the torture that she suddenly craved.

Desperate for a distraction from her brooding thoughts, she climbed carefully onto Snarf's back and pulled out her mother's map. She really needed to figure out how to read this thing, but she had no idea where to begin. She stared at the thick parchment, noting the sketchy drawings, arrows, and unintelligent lettering scattered all over the page. She wondered if the writing was in code or perhaps a different language. She had learned to read while in Cedrick's mansion, but had never encountered symbols like these.

Aleisha was again sitting on Snarf's back, again staring at the chaos of her mother's map. It had been nearly a week since she had learned that she had soul power, but she had avoided every attempt to get a definite answer about whether or not she would learn how to use it. She had spent most of her time staring at the map and wondering which of the three powerful beings she could be. She could draw the stupid map from memory if she tried, but she still had no clue what any of it meant, so she returned, again, to the vision of the mist.

She wanted to believe that the dragon she saw meant that she was a Dragonsoul, but the white mist could have also meant that she was a Lightsoul; she was pretty sure that white mist was often associated with what some of her fellow slaves had called "good magicians." She was now convinced that "good magicians" referred to the gentle Lightsouls that, according to Grezald, often acted as healers in many small towns.

The only really bad option that she could see was also the one that scared her the most. Snarf told her that Darksouls were often corrupted by their power; they would become addicted and use the power and influence they possessed in order to gain more power. She thought of her vision again and remembered the thirst she had felt when the mist began to give her its power; the instant desire for more had scared her when she realized that she understood the addiction.

Aleisha's stomach growled suddenly, reminding her that she had not eaten since the night before, when Snarf had cooked a couple of fennecs for her and Conner. *"Hungry?"* Snarf sounded amused as he asked.

"Humans do eat constantly," Grezald chuckled at his own joke, spurring Grizwald to join with his own obnoxious laughter. Aleisha smiled to herself as she grunted, trying to sound annoyed with the twins' constant play. The two of them had not stopped chasing each other through the sky, or jesting constantly about anything that came up.

"We will soon be approaching the southeastern edge of the desert, so if you can wait a few hours, we will get you something to eat at Puko." When Byron spoke, his deep voice betrayed a small amount of pain as he named the village in the Forest of Karr where his mate had been slain.

Snarf was shooting through the air at speeds that Aleisha had never imagined possible before meeting a dragon; he and the twins were by far the most carefree of the five dragons, and were presently engaged in an intense game of tag. She let out a loud yelp as Grezald swooped a little too close, causing Snarf to have to bank sharply. Even a few days ago, the movement would have caused her to slip, but she had learned quickly to hold tightly to Snarf's fur, especially when Grezald joined the play as he was the most rambunctious of the three, and often did not take her inexperience into account.

She looked beneath them as Snarf made a nose dive and watched the ground grow closer at a speed that should have terrified her, but as they neared the hard sand, he suddenly spread his wings and shot forward, turning them parallel to the ground only a few feet before impact. As the air whipped around her and the loose sand flew about her body, she let out an excited scream. She had never before felt this kind of freedom in her life; she felt completely without limits.

Snarf slowed their flight and began a steady assent, chuckling at her glee. They had left the rest of their party behind, and would now have to wait for them to catch up. This rest provided the perfect opportunity for Aleisha to ask one of the questions that had been plaguing her for days, "Snarf." He turned his head to see her better as she spoke, "Where did magic come from? I've heard that humans didn't always have it."

Snarf hesitated, was it possible that he didn't know? *"Many millennia ago, a war was raging amongst all the nations of Elbot: Ephriat, Belmopan, and Carserin.*

55

Ephriat, the largest, richest, and most powerful army, was decimating Belmopan and Carserin, but the king of Ephriat served an evil god. A mockery actually, a blasphemous spirit named Ban who claimed to be a god.

"The One True God was so angry with the king of Ephriat, that He turned His back on him and refused to aid his people in battle. Belmopan and Carserin were no better; each nation worshiped their own false god and turned their backs on the Creator of their world, and each nation lost the favor of the Lord.

"One young boy, Philimina, had not turned his back on his Creator. He sought the Lord and called on Him to lead the world to peace; all of Elbot was being destroyed by the bloody war and none of the armies showed mercy, even to women and young children. The Lord looked favorably on Philimina and granted his request. The Creator gave the power of the dragons to Philimina to grant to a newborn babe, whom he must train to use the magic to end the war. He chose a boy from the region that is now Might City and trained him until he was a young man. With the help of several dozen dragons, the young magic user led the world to peace.

"After this, the Lord also bestowed another gift on Philimina, the Elixir of Life, which would allow him to live forever and continue to offer the dragon power to a young babe every generation. This was supposed to help keep the world at peace once the war was ended. The Lord warned Philimina not to let anyone else drink the elixir, but he rebelled. He gave the elixir to his friend, Briganti, who drank the elixir and gained eternal life.

"The Lord was enraged with Philimina, and, as punishment, gave the power of the Dictator to both

Briganti and his wife, Zipporah. The power that the Lord gave to Zipporah allowed her to give birth to immortal children; her sons would be Dictators, and her daughters would give birth to Dictators. The power granted to Briganti was the power of what we now call Darksouls.

"By the time Zipporah gave birth to her first daughter, it had become evident that her sons produced much weaker magic users than Philimina or Briganti. In an attempt to correct this unfortunate happening, Philimina granted the dragon power on Zipporah's daughter, Anita, causing her to produce more powerful heirs, this was the start of the Lightsouls. Dissatisfied with this unexpected result, Philimina also granted his power to Anita's final daughter as she died in childbirth. Esther, his new babe, grew tall and beautiful; she had a similar appearance to that of a Lightsoul in true form. When she gave birth to her oldest son, Philimina waited with great anticipation to see if he had succeeded in duplicating the power held by his chosen babe. To his great enjoyment, the young man granted his power to a baby boy and produced only the second Dragonsoul in history.

"During this time, Briganti had also chosen to give his power to one of Zipporah's other daughters, thus creating a line of Darksouls, and a final soul power.

"After several more generations, the Lord ended the creation of Dictators, by this time, there were thousands of them." At this point, the rest of the dragons caught up with them, and Byron and Conner flew next to them. *"I realize that I answered a lot more than you asked, but I hope that cleared up a bit of confusion for you."*

Aleisha thought about what she had just heard for a moment while she stared out at the desert before her. It was amazing that, even though she could only see endless sand in every direction, in less than an hour, they would reach a village surrounded by trees and fed with the icy water of the famous Karr River. She was trying to imagine what it would feel like to bathe in that water after so many days in the hot sun when something occurred to her. "Snarf, isn't Briganti the name of the Dictator in Conner's story?"

"You pay attention," he sounded pleased when he answered her, as if he wondered if she would notice the detail.

"You were at a funeral for Briganti's babe. But why would you be at a funeral for a Darksoul?"

"Aleisha," Conner answered for him, "In spite of his corruption, Briganti is a friend of dragons. We were there to mourn with a friend, not for a Darksoul."

"Did Briganti choose Tallen's child?" Aleisha wasn't sure why she asked with such great urgency, but it seemed important for some reason.

"I don't know for certain who he chose; we haven't been back to Puko since Lorahlie's death." Conner shrugged, as if it wasn't important, "I doubt that he did. Like I said, he is a friend. He knows that to have two Darksouls in the same family could be disastrous, he wouldn't do that to us," he ended in a whisper, as if he wasn't entirely sure of the truth of that statement.

"Aleisha," Snarf interjected enthusiastically, *"look!"* with a nod of his head, Snarf indicated the end of the desert.

The rough sand, which had moments ago seemed endless, slowly gave way to soft, black soil, out of which grew lush green foliage. Shrubs, trees, grasses, and many other plants that Aleisha had never seen before grew so thick that she could not see the brown bark of the trees, or discern where one tree ended and the next started. The beautiful scene reminded her of a painting she had seen the only time she had met her father, the day he sold her to Cedrick.

Her father had never asked to see her before, so her mother had been alarmed when he sent for her two weeks after her fourth birthday. Aleisha remembered her mother screaming after her as she was led out of their cell and down the long hallway toward freedom. She had not understood her mother's worry, thinking that the guards were taking her to live with her father; perhaps he was not as bad as her mother had thought.

The rooms above the dungeon were more spacious and a lot lighter than Aleisha had been accustomed to, and she could still feel the way it had burned her eyes as she adjusted to her bright surroundings. By the time the guard finally stopped walking, Aleisha had developed quite a severe headache, and she could barely force her eyes to remain open. When she looked around the room they had just entered, she gasped at the sight, forgetting her pain as she gazed in awe at her surroundings.

The walls were made of stone, like in her cell, but they were cleaner and stretched at least a dozen feet off the ground, reaching up to a painted ceiling. Each wall had at least one tapestry depicting scenes of war and fire. Artfully crafted wooden chairs sat next to marble pillars that seemed to turn even this large room into a cell. At the far end of the room, between two of the pillars, stood a tall figure, facing away from her, and looking at the most beautiful scene she had ever seen. The many shades of green and blue in the painting captivated the attention of the young girl and filled her imagination with thoughts of running through the field it displayed.

"Aleisha," Conner sounded breathless as he spoke her name, "you've got to stop doing that."

"What?" Aleisha peeled her eyes from the scene in front of her to stare at Conner. She noticed Grizwald looking at her with amazement and some small amount of concern.

"You get distracted easily, when we were riding my horse you did the same thing, you stopped hearing or seeing anything, save your own thoughts." He shook his head slowly, "I should have realized what you were doing."

"She clearly has no idea what you are talking about," Byron turned his head toward Conner as he spoke quietly.

"Did you realize that you were using magic?" Conner directed his question to her as if Byron hadn't spoken.

"No, I couldn't have," she stammered, "I don't even know how."

"We all saw it, Aleisha," Conner spoke slowly, seemingly amazed by what he'd seen. "You were using the sand. You pulled it from the desert floor and built the dungeon, the castle, even the painting with amazing skill." He shook his head again, as if that was the only motion he could perform, "I can't believe that you could do that with no training."

"Are you ready to let us teach you how to control your power?" For the first time, Dagmar sounded sincerely hopeful she would consent to their training.

"It will be safer for all of us if you do," Snarf spoke up, gently urging her to agree, *"You are clearly a very powerful magic user."*

Aleisha thought a moment of her mother, how terrified she was of magicians, and how terrified of her she would be if she ever found out. And what of her father? How terrified she had been in the presence of her father. She wondered if, perhaps, her father was one of the dreaded Darksouls, and if, perhaps, that is why he was so terrible to her and her mother. Maybe her mother would not be afraid of her if she knew that she was not like her father. She would never give anyone a reason to fear her. She would be better than her father. She would be a good magic user. "Yes, I will learn."

Chapter 6

An hour later, Aleisha was climbing down from Snarf's back in the middle of a forest. They had flown above the canopy of trees for several miles before descending into a small clearing. This break in the treetops was the only one she had seen from her perch so high above, and she wondered if it was a natural clearing or if it had been intended as a landing ground for dragons.

She had never before been surrounded by so many plants. Her father's castle had been built in a wide field, covered in grass and flowers, but even the vast green carpet that seemed endless as she rode in the back of Cedrick's wagon could not compare to the dense foliage of the forest. The thick trees that had appeared as nothing more than a huge green blob from above were now clearly defined. Each plant seemed to be a slightly different shade of green, and many of the smaller bushes offered more bursts of color from their vibrant flowers.

As she stared in awe at her surroundings, three men materialized from within the trees. All three wore simple leather pants, and each one had either a bow or a sword secured to a baldric over their otherwise bare torsos. The man in the middle also wore a wolf-skin cape that draped over his shoulders and whipped around his body with the wind. He wore an expression that clearly stated that he was in charge.

Conner moved closer to the men and greeted their leader, who welcomed him with a large smile before turning toward Aleisha, "My name is Ignatius," he held out his arms in a grand gesture, "welcome to our home, it is not often that we receive guests in Puko, but I'm sure you will feel at home in our village." Ignatius then pointed to the men on either side of him, "These are my sons, Garret and Locke." Garret was almost as tall as Conner with an easy smile, while Locke was just barely Aleisha's five-foot-nine, and easily six inches shorter than his brother. Both brothers nodded politely to Aleisha before the whole group turned and disappeared back into the trees.

Conner held a hand out to her, "Stay close, it can be overwhelming at first." He led her towards the trees, pointing out an opening in the bark of one of the larger trees. "We arrived during dinner, so most of the residents will be in the Common Tree." When she stepped inside, the large tree seemed to explode into a huge room of wooden walls and dirt floor. Several bonfires provided light and heat as women stirred various pots over the flames. One older woman handed her spoon to a young girl next to her and rushed over to greet them.

"This is my wife, Fortuna," Ignatius smiled with pride as he introduced the woman. She, as most of the people of Puko, had dark skin and coffee colored hair and was taller than most of the residents of Jaboke, but that only served to make Aleisha feel more comfortable because she, too, was several inches taller than most women she had known.

"What a pleasure," Fortuna smiled excitedly at Aleisha as she moved to grasp Conner's arm, "How many times did I tell you that you just had to be patient?"

Conner smiled at the woman and patted her hand, "It's good to see you again Mater; this is Aleisha." Smirking, he added, "We are not married." Fortuna practically wilted at the statement, losing her beautiful smile for just a moment before perking back up.

"Well," she reached out to grasp Aleisha's arm now, causing her to retract ever so slightly, "I'll just have to keep being patient then."

"Conner," another man appeared next to them, somehow managing to remain unnoticed until that moment. He seemed to be the only person in the common area with lighter skin than Aleisha, a thick white beard grew almost to his chest, further setting him apart from the locals, who all sported clean-shaven faces. The old man spread his arms in welcome, enveloping Conner in a friendly hug before turning to Aleisha. His wide smile instantly turned into a troubled frown that landed somewhere between recognition and worry. She, too, recognized him. She had seen his face dancing in the fire not long ago. This old man was the grieving Dictator, Briganti.

Conner stepped away from Fortuna to lay a hand on Aleisha's shoulder, "This is Aleisha," he lowered his head and added quietly, "she has soul power and we would appreciate your help in teaching her how to control it." Briganti looked almost frightened as Conner spoke, and stared wide-eyed at Aleisha, who was now looking shyly at the ground before his feet. "That is, of course, if it will not be a burden to either you or your babe."

"No, no, my babe doesn't even live with us currently," he continued watching her as he spoke, "Why don't you let her Dictator teach her?" Briganti barely pulled his gaze from her face as he directed his attention to Conner, who slowly shook his head.

"If we knew who her Dictator was, we would go to him, but she has only just recently learned of her magical inclination; whoever claimed her did not do so publicly." The Dictator seemed to relax as Conner spoke, letting out an almost imperceptible sigh.

"Ignatius," he called loudly to the man not three yards behind him, "I will be welcoming Conner and his guest into my home; I trust the dragons' rooms are all in order for them."

"Of course," Ignatius replied grudgingly, seemingly frustrated at being spoken to in such a manner.

Briganti whispered something to Locke, who nodded and hurried away, before motioning for Conner and Aleisha to follow him. He led them out of the common area, stopping for a moment to greet each of the dragons before turning toward a tree just to the right of the Common Tree. Again, Conner pointed out the entrance to the tree, showing her how to spot a doorway before ushering her inside. Much like the Common Tree, this tree had great wooden walls that seemed to stretch ever upward, never revealing a seam or a break. The ceiling appeared only as the ceiling of the forest, thick, dark leaves that hid every spot of sky. Unlike the Common Tree, though, this one was lit with dozens of torches, mounted on the wall in ascending spirals. Following one of the spirals was a wooden staircase carved into the wall of the tree. At several points in the staircase, she could see large hollow caves marking the tree's branches. As they ascended the staircase, she noticed that each of the hollow branches had been transformed into a living area, and each one was furnished with a desk, chair, wardrobe, and bed all made out of various kinds of wood. The room lowest on the tree was furnished with rich cherry wood and had a few paintings, a potted shrub, and a bookshelf that gave the area a feeling of home, but most of the other rooms were mostly bare, as if set up to accommodate guests in an inn.

Briganti led Conner and Aleisha up the staircase and past a few of the rooms before stopping at one with sturdy oak furnishings and a vase of wildflowers on the desk. A single torch was mounted directly above the desk, casting a warm glow about the entire room. A curtain of ivy had been secured to the wall by a hook and could be let down to offer some privacy to the tenant. As Aleisha looked curiously about the room, she heard Briganti and Conner speaking quietly behind her.

"If I had my guess," Conner's voice was almost silent as he addressed his friend, "I would say that she is a Dragonsoul; she is very powerful."

"A magic user with any soul power is very powerful," Briganti responded just as quietly, "She could just as easily be a Darksoul."

"No," Conner's voice came more forcefully now, "she does not have enough evil in her to be a Darksoul."

"My dear Conner, everyone has enough evil in them," the Dictator sounded like he was correcting a child, "Darksouls simply know how to harness that evil and turn it into raw power."

Aleisha turned toward her companions and reclaimed her place at Conner's side. She didn't appreciate

Briganti's suggestion that she could be a Darksoul; she would bet that he only said it because of his own affiliation with the horrid creatures. Briganti pasted his smile back into place as he nodded to Aleisha and spoke directly to her, "This will be your room while I train you, but I should warn you that that could take quite some time." Briganti pointed to the desk and the wardrobe, "You will find that all you need has been provided." With that, he turned to leave. Conner was still glaring at him when he had completely disappeared down the steps.

"Conner," Aleisha spoke for the first time since entering Puko.

"Yes?" he turned toward her and she noticed for the first time that he looked rather tired, perhaps from their trip, but more likely from his argument with Briganti; it was never an enjoyable thing to fight with a friend.

"This tree did not look so large outside, how is it so huge?"

"It's magic," Conner looked again toward the steps, "Briganti came to live in Puko over a century ago with his chosen babe at the time. The Darksoul transformed the way the people of Puko lived when he enchanted the trees."

"Why would such an evil creature as a Darksoul do something so helpful for them?"

"Even Darksouls need a place to live," Conner shook his head and turned toward her, again revealing the tired expression on his face, "you will likely find that every Darksoul you run into provides extravagant wealth and protection for the people with whom he dwells. Because of this, he is well loved in his home; he would not be welcome otherwise." He turned to the stairs and indicated a hollowed-out branch on the other side of the tree, "If you need me, I'll be right over there. You will likely be brought your dinner today, but we'll be expected to join the common area for breakfast, so I'll come get you in the morning."

With those final words, he exited, leaving Aleisha to explore her new home. She wandered over to her desk and opened her drawer. Inside, she discovered a small mirror, an ivory brush, a few pieces of parchment, and a quill with a bottle of ink. Gathering the brush and mirror, she placed them on the desk for easy access and headed to the wardrobe, in which she found several articles of clothing, mostly black and brown, but one lone off-white dress was tucked carefully in the back of the closet. Picking a simple brown dress, she placed it on the bed and headed to the entrance to close her ivy curtain.

"Aleisha," Fortuna called from a few steps below, holding a tray of food, "I have brought you dinner." She smiled kindly as she breezed past her into the room. "Ah, did the wardrobe not offer night clothes?" she nodded toward the dress on the bed as she placed the tray on the desk. Aleisha had not thought to check the drawers for night clothes as she had never had a separate outfit for sleeping, she had always slept in her work dress, leaving her nicer clothes unrumpled so as to not displease Cedrick. "I can have some brought for you later if you like. I'm sure you will be wanting a warm bath as well, nothing like a good soak after a long journey." The matronly woman smiled again as she looked her over. "You have a strong build. You come from a life of work."

"I do," she wasn't sure how much she should share with this woman that she did not know, but she seemed friendly, so she tried not to judge her too harshly; the people of Puko had no way of knowing that she was a runaway slave.

"Eat. You must be starving." Gesturing toward the food she had brought, Fortuna sat on the edge of Aleisha's bed. She clearly had no intention of leaving, so Aleisha claimed her chair and began tearing into her food. She had forgotten how hungry she was, but as soon as the warm bread touched her tongue, she sighed in pleasure and began shoving food in her mouth in a very unladylike manner. "I see I was right," Fortuna laughed at her rudeness, but somehow managed to keep from sounding condescending as she did. Maybe this woman really was as kind as she seemed; she was certainly friendly enough. "Do you mind me asking how you came to know Conner? He's very dear to me and my husband, and we're so glad to see him befriend another human." Again, she sounded nothing but kind, as if she meant only what she said and nothing more. Aleisha wasn't quite sure how to respond to that, as every woman she had ever known either treated her with distaste for being a slave or with contempt for being the favorite.

"Um," she slowly lowered her bowl of stew that she had been drinking, looking for a safe answer, "We met in a city south of here, we were headed in the same direction, so we teamed up," it wasn't the whole truth, but she didn't know this woman and didn't see a need to explain further. "Why did you say you're glad he befriended a human? Does he not usually?"

"Oh, Conner just tends to stick with his dragon friends and leave it at that," she folded her hands and sighed, "he's always felt more comfortable with them, at least as long as I've known him." She suddenly jumped up from the bed and hurried over to the doorway, apparently hearing something as she held the curtain even farther out of the way for a large man to enter. She recognized Garret as he entered, carrying the front end of a large metal bathtub. He and Locke silently followed their mother's instructions as they placed the tub by one of the walls. Fortuna ushered the men out and reached for a perfectly round knot hole positioned just a couple of feet above the tub. "How warm do you like your bath?" she turned to look at Aleisha for a moment before chuckling and reaching her hand into the knot, "I'll make it hot, and you can wait for it to cool if you like." As if responding to her words, water began pouring from the hole in the wall and splashing into the tub below, filling it with steaming liquid. "I'll just leave you to your dinner then. You can leave the tray and the bath when you're finished with them, I'll have someone take care of them tomorrow; you must be absolutely exhausted." Smiling one last time, she left the room and hurried down the stairs.

Aleisha tiptoed over to the bath, peering inside with curiosity and wonder as the stream of hot water slowed to a drizzle before finally stopping altogether. She carefully dipped her finger into the water, testing the temperature before rushing over to the curtain to let down the ivy. With that small amount of privacy restored, she undressed, thinking how lovely it felt to shed the clothes that she had been wearing for over a week. As soon as the fabric dropped to the floor, she pulled the ribbon from her long hair and, draping it over her shoulder, stepped into the hot water, lowering her body into the refreshing liquid.

Chapter 7

Aleisha opened her eyes and yawned noisily. She could not remember having ever slept so comfortably, even the soft wings of a dragon could not compare with the cool, soft mattress on which she now lie. Stretching her arms above her head, she pushed herself out of the bed and reached for the dress that was still draped over the end of the bed from the night before. The brown dress was a simple design with an emphasis on functionality rather than beauty. It had pockets on either side of the skirt and wide sleeves that could easily be pushed aside if needed. She marveled at how well it fit her, as no dress had ever fit her thin, long form without special tailoring.

She had just finished brushing her hair when she heard the ivy curtain rustle behind her. "Very fitting for a magic user," Conner smiled and nodded approvingly. "You can begin training after breakfast." She grinned at that. No man had ever looked at her like that before, with neither desire nor distaste. She wondered if this was how free women were treated, or if this was simply how Conner treated women.

Conner led her back to the Common Tree. Just like the night before, the area was full of people gathering around small fires, preparing various breakfast foods. Fortuna came running to them to greet them, enveloping Conner in a welcoming hug. "Mornin' Mater," he smiled down at the older woman, taking her arm in his as she led them to her family's fire pit.

"Conner and Aleisha will be joining us." Ignatius, Garret, and Locke were all standing near the fire, speaking quietly with Briganti, when Fortuna made the announcement. Garret immediately turned to glare at Conner with a look of pure hatred in his eyes.

"Of course," Ignatius smiled at them and moved to greet Conner as Fortuna had, before turning to Aleisha, "I trust you slept well."

"I did, thank you." She was grateful that he did not try to hug her, as he had Conner; she was not comfortable in her new surroundings as it was. She glanced around the group, noting two other women and a few small children, most likely the families of Garret and Locke.

"We will begin your training after breakfast," Briganti smiled at Aleisha, apparently eager to begin.

"I think she is ready to learn," Conner nodded at the old man as he placed a hand on her shoulder, "but you may find it difficult to teach her."

Briganti chuckled at that, "And why would that be?"

"She has already begun to use her power unconsciously," came the quiet reply, "She doesn't even know when she's doing it."

"You wield a very powerful magic indeed Aleisha," he leaned close to her, so that only she could hear, "Perhaps you belong to one of the original three." Briganti's smile never faltered as he stared at her, though his eyes did harden into a look suspiciously similar to greed. She shivered as her whole body suddenly flashed cold. She unconsciously stepped closer to Conner, sensing that Briganti desired to control her and not wanting to be near him unnecessarily. His suggestion that she might be a Darksoul coupled with this mysterious comment seemed to suggest he had a more personal motivation than Conner's request to train her.

"Aleisha," Fortuna drew her back into the conversation. She had to learn to stay more focused; it had never been a problem when working for Cedrick because no one expected her to follow a conversation, but now she was finding herself constantly being drawn back into a conversation that she had carelessly exited. "Could you help me get drinks for the men?"

"Of course," she smiled at the older woman, prepared to follow her before suddenly being flanked by Garret and Locke.

"We'll help her, Mater. You should let us serve you more often." Garret spoke kindly to his mother as he gripped Aleisha's arm to lead her away from the group. Conner did not look pleased by their offer but remained silent.

"It has been a long time since Briganti has had a chosen babe here in Puko," Locke spoke as soon as they were out of earshot of the others, "It will be twenty-five years this fall that his last one died. I wonder who he chose to replace him." By the tone of his voice, Aleisha didn't think he wondered at all; he thought he had already figured it out. He was wrong though, Aleisha could not possibly be Briganti's chosen babe. She may be the right age, but she was not evil enough to be a Darksoul and she would not allow Locke to accuse her of such a thing.

"I have no way of knowing who Briganti would have chosen," she stopped and turned to the leader's son, yanking her arm from Garret's grip as she did so. "All I can say for sure is that I have never met his chosen

74

babe." It was only then that it occurred to her how odd his statement was. He said that Briganti's last babe died twenty-five years ago, but Conner was at Gabriel's funeral and had already been a grown man at that time.

"We have missed having a magic user in our presence," Garret continued from beside her as if she hadn't spoken, "I was only a boy when Gabriel died, but I remember he was quite a pleasant fellow, even the livestock liked him."

"I was not yet born when he died, so I don't remember him." Locke gave Aleisha a sneer as he said this and added quietly, "or Conner, for that matter. This is the first time he's been back since the funeral." She didn't know what to say to that, clearly, he meant to say that Conner was much older than he appeared, and while he had never come out and stated that he was her age, she felt as if he had intentionally deceived her. Unless it was Garret and Locke who were deceiving her; after all, Briganti's babe could very easily still be in diapers, and these men were only trying to harm her friendship with Conner based on their obvious disdain for him. But how could they have guessed her age so accurately? "Briganti did seem happy to see you, almost as if he were reuniting with a lost loved one."

"Enough!" Aleisha saw the fire in the pits grow momentarily fiercer as she barked at him. Several of the women tending to cooking pots yelped in alarm as the high flames engulfed their dishes, and she could not help feel some small amount of satisfaction at Locke's stunned expression.

"Aleisha," Conner suddenly appeared behind her, placing his hand on her back. She hoped that he did not hear their absurd accusations. "I think you men can handle getting the drinks without Aleisha." Both men glared at Conner, hatred burning in the eyes of both men, but after a moment, they turned and continued the direction they had been leading her. "They hate me, Aleisha." He whispered, "Our relationship causes them to hate you as well, so you should avoid being alone with either of them; you would regret allowing them to provoke you." She just nodded and allowed him to lead her back to the fire pit.

"Your horse arrived early this morning," Ignatius laughed as they neared them, "I will never understand how you get your animals to do that." Conner only smiled in response and sat next to Fortuna.

She had never seen such luxury! Even growing up enjoying Cedrick's riches, she could not have dreamed such food to be so readily available. After eating her fill of various meats, gravies, and breads, Aleisha excused herself from the group to find Snarf before her training began. Conner directed her to the meadow just outside the Common Tree, where she found all five dragons contentedly purring after having finished their own large breakfast. *"Are you enjoying your visit to Puko, Aleisha?"* the dragon seemed unwaveringly concerned for her wellbeing; it was a nice change from her life of servitude.

"I actually have a few questions, if you don't mind," It occurred to her that she could say anything she wanted to Snarf and he would forgive any misstep along the way, *"How long has it been since you've been here?"*

"We have not been here since Lorahlie's death," Snarf's expression told her that he knew this was not a satisfactory answer, so he tried again, *"I do not keep track of years well, but I think it has been somewhere between twenty and thirty; all the young children I remember are now fully-grown adults."*

"So, Conner is much older than he appears."

"That was for your benefit, Aleisha," he snickered as he spoke, shaking his head slightly. *"We did not want him to scare you."*

"How old is he then?" She could not believe what she was hearing. She remembered thinking that he looked about twenty years older in the story, but that estimation would put him at almost eighty.

"Why does it matter? Magic can allow a fellow to live a very long time, and, like I said, time keeping has never been my strong point. I'm not even sure I can tell you how old I am." The way he addressed the issue made it sound unimportant. He almost made her feel silly for asking, but she felt she at least needed to know if Locke had been right about the timing of Gabriel's death,

She thought about asking Byron if he knew how long it had been, but decided against it when she realized how tactless it would be to bring up such a painful memory in the very place where she had died, *"Grizwald, do you know how many years it has been since you have been here?"*

"It will be twenty-five years this autumn. Why?" Grizwald answered her as he chewed lazily on a large reed.

"Ignatius' son said something about it and it seemed strange that it could have been so long ago."

77

"What does she want?" Dagmar's voice broke into the conversation quite unexpectedly; she wondered why he even let her hear him, though she suspected that it was just out of spite.

"She's just expressing her undying curiosity. Nothing you shouldn't expect by now." It pleased her how nonchalant Grizwald sounded as he answered his older brother, who grunted in response.

"I was actually wondering if you could explain something else to me as well," she tried to proceed with as much caution as she could; she did not want to upset her new friends if her questions became a nuisance to them. At Snarf's patient expression, she decided that it was safe to continue, "Briganti mentioned something about the 'original three.' Do you know what that means?"

"He was talking about the most powerful Dictators," Snarf looked to Byron, who nodded.

"You will remember that Snarf told you about Philimina, the original Dictator," Aleisha nodded to show him that she did, *"he is the most powerful Dragonsoul Dictator and so, consequently, his chosen babe is the most powerful Dragonsoul. The same is true of Briganti, the original Darksoul Dictator, and Felix, Anita's oldest child and first Lightsoul Dictator."*

"Why did he mention the original three? He wasn't bragging, was he?" Grizwald snickered as he said this, but his voice held a hint of seriousness.

"He said that I was powerful enough that I could belong to one of the original three," As soon as she said it, she wished she hadn't. Dagmar gave her a look that suggested he was trying to decide how well he wanted her cooked when he ate her, Grezald looked worried, and Byron, Snarf, and Grizwald looked angry.

"He was trying to upset you. He knows very well that you cannot be as he says," Byron spoke quietly, as if trying to cover his rage, *"He personally knows Philimina's child, and has seen him alive and well too recently for you to have come after him and Felix just chose a new babe a few months ago, which means that he was insinuating that you would have to be his babe; something that you could not have known without asking us. Clearly, he is angry with us for failing to visit since Lorahlie's murder and is trying to upset us."*

Aleisha decided that it would be wise to remain silent for a while after such an emotional response from Byron, but it seemed to her that, if Briganti wanted to upset them, he wouldn't have whispered his comment to her. She worried that he had meant what he said, but could it be true that she was a Darksoul? The timing certainly worked, but why would he have chosen a babe born in captivity? All she could know for certain was that she would never act like a Darksoul, whether she was one or not. No one else would get to choose whether she would be good or evil; that was her choice.

Chapter 8

Aleisha had been sitting with Snarf for almost an hour after she had finished eating breakfast. She sat quietly, listening to the dragons tell stories of times that they had been here in the past. From what she could tell, Puko had been a favorite visiting place for several hundred years, and the people had always treated the dragons as honored guests, welcoming them with feasts and building them a special dwelling even before Gabriel had given them the magic to make building large homes easier.

After listening to a particularly entertaining story from Grezald about a hunting trip that he had taken one of the woodmen on as a young boy, Aleisha saw Briganti walking toward her.

As soon as she saw him, her back stiffened and she glared at the Dictator; she did not like the old man and was not particularly looking forward to being taught by him. As he neared, the dragon voices in her head ceased and she could have sworn she heard one of them growl softly. A smile stretched across his leathery face but did not reach his eyes as he stopped just feet away from her. "Are you ready to begin, Aleisha?" the look in his eyes sent shivers down her spine, but she stood and faced him, stretching to her full height, which, much to her delight, put her several inches above him.

"Of course," she spoke with a dignity that she did not feel; she dreaded having to be alone with him, and she guessed that he would not allow anyone to observe her training.

80

Briganti led her out of the village and up a steep incline to a small hill. It looked like there had been trees at one point, but none grew now. The area seemed to pulse with the same power that she had felt in her strange vision when she first learned that she was a magic user. "How is it that I could have gone so long without knowing that I had magic?" she had not intended to ask the question aloud, and so was slightly surprised when Briganti answered her.

"Your Dictator never claimed you, even after he chose you, so you did not grow with the knowledge of your power that most would have. Because of this, your magic was awakened when you felt safe enough to discover it." He turned to her then and, seeing her confused expression, added, "Tell me, did you feel safe in Cedrick's mansion, or were you always a little bit guarded?"

"How do you know about that?"

"It's not hard to guess that you did not feel comfortable in…"

"You know that's not what I meant," Aleisha cut him off midsentence and sent him a glare that would have turned a campfire into ice.

"Oh, of course," he replied to her glare with another of his infuriating smiles, "Conner told me you had been a slave."

"Conner did not know the name of my former master. I have not spoken that snake's name since leaving his mansion. How did you know his name?"

She could see the haughty look in his eyes disappear like a thin vapor, as he tried to quickly form his next lie. After a moment of silence, he smiled again and spoke, but this time he sounded completely sincere, "I've kept a pretty close watch on you since I chose you. I had been planning to take you away from Cedrick as soon as you discovered your ability; I had not been expecting it to take so long."

"I'm not a Darksoul," even as she spoke, she never relaxed her threatening posture; she refused to easily believe a man whom she had discovered to be lying to her not a moment ago.

"Are you quite sure though?" he had adopted the tone of a teacher patiently explaining an important lesson to his student. "Every soul power holds a unique ability; it is one of the things that differentiate one from the others. Dragonsouls are the only human beings capable of unassisted flight, Lightsouls can transform their bodies and adopt the image of an animal, and Darksouls, as I'm sure you've discovered, can hear the telepathic conversations of the dragons around them even if they are not invited to."

"Ha, I've never heard a word that I was not supposed to," but even as her voice escaped her lips, she thought of hearing Snarf arguing with Conner, even after he had fallen silent. She remembered Dagmar's rude comment after breakfast and wondered if he had meant for her to hear him. She remembered all the half conversations she had heard between Conner and one of the dragons while they flew toward Puko.

"You have heard many things you were not meant to hear; I can see by the look in your eyes that you know what I say to be true. The first time a dragon allows you to hear its voice, it can never hide from you again, though they will most certainly try." Briganti paused, letting her remember dozens of times she had heard things and thought it odd that she had been allowed in the conversation. "You must never let them know that you can hear them, surely you know the hate Conner and his winged brothers have for your kind. Surely you have heard the story of Tallen. Surely they have told you what your father did to Byron's precious mate."

Aleisha jerked her head back to look at Briganti again. He could not possibly be telling the truth. She did not know her father's name, but could he really be Tallen? She had previously wondered if her father could be a Darksoul, but the idea that he might actually be one was too horrifying to believe, and the thought that Tallen could be her father was entirely unacceptable. "You are quite tall, Aleisha, just like your father." He sneered.

"Prove it." She could feel her entire body shake as the rage begged to be released, "Prove that Tallen is my father."

"How can I? Do I have magic that I can use to show you his image?" he seemed to be enjoying watching her fume. The expression on his face suggested that he had just experienced a great success. He had just angered her. He had just introduced her to a Darksoul's greatest weapon: hatred. "Why don't you ask Byron to show Tallen to you? I'm sure he remembers what he looks like." She would not stand here and listen to his manipulation and lies any longer. She spun away from him and marched out of the clearing.

Aleisha moved like smoke through the forest, taking the exact path she had traveled with Briganti to return to the village. She was furious, and her magic seemed to feed on the fury, gliding her over rocks, sticks, and roots without her ever needing to think about it. She would not believe what Briganti said about Tallen, but she would speak with one of the dragons about him. Maybe she would ask Snarf or Grizwald, all she had decided for certain was that she would not be so cruel as to ask Byron, and she would not be so stupid as to ask Dagmar, that would only give him more reason to hate her.

As she neared Puko, she saw two young men, covered in dirt and carrying bows, run past her silently. She heard a small animal, possibly a rabbit, run through the greenery beside her. Several large birds sat quietly on a branch somewhere above her head, watching for dinner to come scurrying by. All these things she felt, more than observed, as she allowed the power she felt growing stronger with every breath show her the world in a way she had never imagined it before. It was as if she was a part of the forest around her and knew, much as her hands knew when her feet were moving, exactly what was happening in the trees around her.

By the time she reached the clearing, she could almost feel the young seedlings trying to grow in the dirt under her, and she wondered if she could ever return to her unseeing state of ignorance after feeling the forest as she did now.

Conner was by her side almost before she entered the meadow at the center of Puko. "I'm sorry," he spoke with an urgency that she did not understand, "I should not have allowed him to have you alone the first time. I should have come with you."

"Why?" she turned to him, wondering what he knew, afraid of what she would do to him if he made the same accusations that Briganti had. "Why should you have come with me? What did you expect him to do?"

"Briganti is a Darksoul Dictator, so I should have considered that he would try to teach you like he does Darksouls." He shook his head slightly and reached for her hand, offering her some small amount of comfort in his touch, "He has always taught that anger is the best fuel for magic, which is part of the reason that Darksouls are corrupt. He is, in a sense, the leader of the Darksouls. I should have thought that he would try to upset you, I'm sorry."

"Is he right?" Conner seemed disappointed that she had asked, and she felt his grip on her hand loosen ever so slightly.

"No," he sighed, "magic is like the body, it can be fueled with any emotion; if a man is angry enough, he can break through a wall, or if he is afraid, he runs faster than he would have thought possible. It works the same with magic, if you become angry or scared, your magic will experience a temporary boost." Aleisha grunted and stared at the ground, between fear and anger, she would prefer anger; she was tired of being afraid. "Aleisha," Conner spoke softly this time and gently lifted her head to look in her eyes, "love has always been a greater motivator than hate. A person acting to serve others rather than themselves will better be able to control the emotional boost their power receives. This is not just the teaching of the Dragonsouls and Lightsouls, but also of the Creator. He never intended us to live in hate, but commands us to serve others." With a pleading look in his eyes, he stared at her a few moments, as if willing her to understand.

"I need to find Snarf. Do you know where he is?" she could tell that this was not what he wanted to hear, but all she cared about right now was finding the truth about her father. With a final squeeze, he let her hand drop, and pointed behind him with his thumb.

"Just go into the big tree, Snarf usually stays in the small branch near the top."

Nodding once, Aleisha headed toward the large tree that she recognized as the dragons' dwelling place in Conner's story. The inside of the tree seemed to be almost identical to Briganti's home, except that everything was bigger, save the staircase, which seemed to be only for the use of visitors as she could see her winged friends flying easily from branch to branch. She did not look forward to the long climb up the enormous tree, but she was determined to speak with Snarf as soon as she could.

Placing her foot on the first step, she thought about what Conner had said about the Creator not wanting her to live in hate. If Tallen turned out to be her father, she could not be sure it was possible not to hate him, much less to serve him as Conner had suggested. She had difficulty enough forgiving him for what he did to her mother, but if he had murdered Gabriel in order to have her chosen for power and murdered Byron's mate because of a simple spell, she did not think that she could, or even wanted to forgive him for those things.

She looked up to see how far she had left to climb and found, to her great surprise, that she was already half way up. She had barely felt the assent as she had been focused solely on her thoughts. She wondered how Snarf would react to her request; she was sure he would show her what she needed, but she did not want him to suspect what Briganti had alleged. She needed only to see Tallen's face to be able to confirm or reject Briganti's claim; though she had only seen her father's face one time, she had never forgotten him.

She reached a large branch that had been hollowed out like her room, but it had no wooden furnishings like hers. In one corner was a large pile of grasses and straw, she presumed that that would be Snarf's bed, and in the other was a single torch, shedding a soft glow on a shallow pool filled with water. What she did not see was a dragon, she knew, though she was not sure how she knew, that this was Snarf's room, but she did not see him either in the room or flying about the rest of the tree. Cautiously, she entered the room and headed toward the bed, intending to sit and wait for her friend, but as she neared the pile of grass, she heard a snort behind her.

"I take it your training did not go well," Snarf's gentle voice suggested sympathy for what Briganti had said to her, even though she knew that he had no way of knowing what it was. *"I should have warned you that he would try to elicit an emotional response from you, but I felt that you, if anyone, would be able to handle his taunting."* Aleisha wondered why he would say that; he had only known her for a little over a week. How could he have such confidence in her already? *"Did you come to discuss what he said to you?"*

"Do you know what he said?" she whirled around and shot him a glair, surprised to see the torch on the other side of the room drop into the pool below, sending the room into darkness.

"You must learn to control your anger, Aleisha, or you will inevitably hurt someone you care about," his patient voice betrayed no offence at her accusation. Had he been expecting it? *"I do not know what he said to you, I only know that he said whatever he thought would anger you the most."*

"So, what he said was a calculated lie?"

"Not necessarily, you will find, as he did many centuries ago, that the truth has more power to elicit a response than a lie ever will." He walked over to the pool to fish out the torch with his great paw, blowing it off with his warm breath, and relit it. *"You came to me for a reason, what was it?"*

She paused before answering him, not sure how to breach the subject without giving away what he had said to her. If Tallen was her father, she did not want anyone to know; Conner and his dragons would surely hate her, and she would lose something much more precious to her than the chance to find the elixir. She would not stand for the idea of losing their friendship.

"We spoke briefly about the day that Lorahlie was murdered. Briganti suggested that I had met Tallen before, while my father had me and my mother locked in a cell." She told herself that it was not a lie, because she had met her father only once, when she was living in her cell. "I was wondering if you could show me what he looked like so that I can know if he was lying to me."

Snarf seemed bothered by her request, but he nodded slowly and summoned her to come closer to the pool. *"A dragon's memory is almost perfect, but I saw him without his hood only once, so the image may not be flawless."*

88

The water in the pool swirled and bent, much like the flame did the first time she saw Tallen. This time, though, she would see his face. She could see a man materializing before her, taking shape and hardening into a solid form. He wore the same cloak as the last time she saw him, but it did not hide his face this time; his pale skin, dark eyes, and cruel sneer were on full display, and she could see the scar on his face where, her mother had told her, he had been hit with an arrow he was not quick enough to deflect with his magic. Every part of his face was the exact image she remembered from the castle. This man, no this monster, was her father. She was the baby that Tallen had offered to Briganti twenty-five years ago.

"Do you recognize him?" Snarf's voice broke through her thoughts, and it occurred to her that her hatred must have been evident in her expression.

"No." She felt sick as soon as the lie left her lips, but she could not bear to see the look on Snarf's face if she told him the truth, if she told him that she was a Darksoul. "I hate him though, for what he did to Byron, to Lorahlie." That, at least, was truth. She did not hate her father for anything he did to her; she had long since come to peace about her past and felt nothing, good or evil, toward the man who had imprisoned her from birth and sold her into slavery. He had seen her as livestock, and she saw him as a cattle trader. But she had nothing but disgust for the man who had caused such pain for her friends. She hated him for what he did to Lorahlie. She hated him for making Conner and the dragons hate Darksouls. She hated him because now, because he had given her to Briganti, she would have to hide herself from the only friends she had ever had.

Chapter 9

Aleisha sat in the chair by her desk, staring at her reflection in the small mirror. She had always hated being told that she had to smile, because her smile was only another asset that Cedrick had loved to show off to his rich and powerful friends and colleagues, but now she wished that she could remember how to bury all her feelings inside and paste her perfect smile into place. It seemed that the only expression her muscles could remember how to create was an angry scowl.

"Byron told me he saw you climbing the staircase," Conner's voice startled her, and she almost dropped the mirror, "Did talking to Snarf help?"

"Not really, I'm not sure talking can help at all." She turned to him then, seeing that he was easily leaning on her doorway with one foot crossed over the other. He looked so relaxed, so comfortable, so young. "How old are you?"

She could see that she had taken him by surprise, but he looked amused, rather than upset, by the question, "Over a hundred, why?"

"Snarf mentioned that magic could make you live a long life; I was just wondering how long."

He nodded at that, "As a magic wielder, your lifespan will mostly depend on what Dictator you have. The more powerful the Dictator, the longer your life can be." He pushed away from the wall then and walked toward her. "All magic wielders have the potential to live to two or three hundred. Maybe even older, depending on who your Dictator is."

"Is there any way to figure that out?"

"If you really want to find out, you'd have to start with figuring out what soul power you have." He stood right beside her now, his tall form towering over her as she sat, slightly slumped, in her chair.

"How would I do that?"

"Well," he sat on the edge of her desk and rubbed the back of his neck, "You could try wielding each of the three unique soul power abilities. I've never heard of it being done, as Dictators usually claim their chosen babe, but you could always try I guess. For instance, if you are a Dragonsoul, you should be able to fly. Some young Dragonsouls will throw themselves from a cliff to force themselves to change into their true form for the first time so that they can save themselves." He laughed then, as if remembering witnessing a young Dragonsoul flying for the first time."

"But you said that I have to know already what power I have before I can change,"

"That's true. I suppose we could try ruling the other options out, though," he smiled before continuing, "For instance, we know you cannot be a Darksoul, because Darksouls can hear the telekinetic conversations of anyone who has let themselves be heard by them. So, since you haven't heard every word spoken in the last week, we know you aren't a Darksoul." She had been hoping Briganti was lying about that; now she knew she was a Darksoul.

"Wait, then why did Lorahlie speak to Tallen when he came to Puko? Was that before you knew what he could do?"

He shook his head, staring intently at a spot on the floor, "She had spoken to him years before when she saw him near the temple of Ban, the false god. She had been looking for a priest that needed to be brought to justice for some heinous crimes against a young girl and did not realize that she was addressing a Darksoul. After realizing who he was, it was too late for her to hide her voice again, so she did not bother trying." At her worried expression, he spoke again, "What is bothering you, Aleisha? What did Briganti say to you?"

"I don't want him to teach me how to use my magic," she stared him in the eyes, willing him to let her change the subject. "I want to learn from one of the dragons"

"Ok, but you may find it difficult to learn from dragons; they don't use magic the same way we do. For them, it's like speaking or walking, a natural part of their existence designed as part of who they are. For us, magic is directly connected to our emotions; that was the safest way the Creator could have given it to us so that it does not interfere with our normal bodily functions. That's why you tend to use magic when you reminisce about things in your past, or when you get upset."

"But I can learn from a dragon?"

He looked thoughtful as he weighed his words before speaking again, "I will speak with them. I'm sure Byron will understand your request, but I will not promise a favorable answer." He clapped his hands together and smiled again, "Now, for a more pleasant topic of conversation: Fortuna asked me to find out your favorite meal."

She smiled at that remembering the sweet woman, "I really don't have one," he shrugged and moved to stand, "Why do you call her Mater?"

"It means mother," he looked so sweet as he said it, "she took me into her house when I needed a place to stay, and she has been more a mother to me than I have ever had, despite being young enough to be my granddaughter." He laughed and shook his head, smiling affectionately.

"Her sons don't seem pleased by that."

"No," he scoffed, "Locke, especially, takes offence that his mother would call me 'son.' He was weeks away from birth last time I was here, so I'm sure that my arrival feels like an unwelcome addition to the family."

"She seems a lovely woman," she thought of her welcoming manner and sweet attitude toward Conner. "I've never felt so easily accepted before."

"Yes," he laughed again, "she has always been a bit too eager for me to get married; she was very excited to see you traveling with me." He shook his head in amusement, "She'll probably make a few more unsubtle comments before we leave, making clear her hopes."

"Oh," she had heard Conner make a comment when they first arrived about them not being married, but she had been so distracted at the time, that she had barely noticed, "Why haven't you married? Is it because of your constant traveling?"

"I was going to," he looked suddenly serious, and cleared his throat before continuing, "My fiancée was killed because of the betrayal of a mutual friend; I haven't pursued anyone since." He looked so forlorn, so hurt, that Aleisha wondered for a moment if he was going to cry, but he took a deep breath and stood up, no sign of sadness remaining. "I'm going to read for a while before dinner." When he reached the ivy curtain, he turned toward her once more, "Don't let the sun go down while you are still angry, Aleisha." With that, he left.

She knew he was right; she had heard since she was small that going to bed angry would cause her to become bitter, punishing her more than the person she was angry with. She had thought it a silly notion, the idea that one would punish themselves over something someone else did, but right now she understood. She wanted to remain angry at Tallen and Briganti. Part of her wanted to be angry at Conner and Byron because she couldn't tell them why she was mad, but she knew that that was foolish. She stared again at her reflection, forcing her muscles into a smile until she could see her eyes begin to soften. If Conner could speak about his fiancée without a hint of anger, she could let go of her anger toward the men in her life. If not for herself, she could at least do so for Conner.

Gazing at the wall in front of her, she tried to think of something pleasant to distract her from all the frustrations of the day. She settled on the first conversation she had with Snarf, focusing on remembering how she felt when she heard his magical voice for the first time. She remembered how impressed he had been that Conner had deemed her worthy of his trust. She could almost hear his words echo in her memory, *"Conner doesn't even allow his Dictator to speak with us anymore."*

She jumped out of her chair, hearing it crash to the floor behind her as she ran out of the room. How had she not figured it out before? How could she have missed that he was a magic user? As she climbed the stairs, she thought of all the signs she'd missed: his instant sweating on the horse, the dancing flames as he told the story of Lorahlie and Tallen, he had several times even made comments about her joining them if she were a Dragonsoul. But she hadn't missed them. When they first met, she knew that he had magic, but he had denied it. No, he had denied being a magician. She stopped and let her mouth drop, unable to believe what she had just discovered, unable to believe that she hadn't figured it out earlier.

When she reached Conner's room, she paused for only a second before entering without knocking, reasoning that he hadn't knocked any time he had entered her room. Maybe he considered it unnecessary. "You're a Dragonsoul."

He looked up from his book with a startled expression, grinning after a second, "How'd you figure it out?"

"Tallen called you 'dragon boy,' I heard you talking with Byron about welcoming me into the family if I was a Dragonsoul, you denied being a magician and then said those with soul power would be offended if I called them that." She started toward him, excitement at her discovery building as she spoke, "Snarf mentioned your Dictator the first time we met; I didn't realize what that meant, but now," she stopped then, not sure how to continue. By Conner's expression, she didn't need to.

"I was wondering how long it would take you to figure it out," he nodded and scratched his neck, "I admit I was not expecting you to figure out I was a Dragonsoul though. I'm impressed." He stood and offered the chair to her, taking a seat on the desk, as he had in her room. He appeared to be concentrating on something at his feet as he stared, unseeing, at the floor. "I don't make a habit of telling people about my power," he looked at her then, willing her to understand, "I hope you aren't offended by my omission."

She could only stare at him, wondering what else she would discover about him before she really knew him. She understood why he would keep his power a secret; it could be dangerous to reveal yourself as a magic user in certain parts of Ephriat. She even understood why he would keep it from her specifically, knowing that her magic wielding father had sold her into slavery. She could see no reason to be offended by him, knowing that he had just as likely failed to reveal himself for her sake as for his. After all, wasn't she keeping her secret to keep him from hating her?

They stared at each other for a long time before Conner finally moved to Aleisha and crouched in front of her, "Do you know what time it is?" he whispered, to which she shook her head. "It's almost time for dinner, so I think we should head down to the Common Tree," he smiled then and stood to help her out of her seat, "You can continue uncovering all of my secrets after we eat."

Chapter 10

Aleisha woke the next morning to see a pair of big brown eyes. A small child had found her way into the room and had made herself comfortable on Aleisha's pillow. "Hello," she sat up slowly and addressed the girl, who was watching her like she was some strange creature she had never seen before. When she didn't answer, she tried again, "What's your name?"

"Kailey," the girl sat up, mimicking Aleisha's movement, even tilting her head in the same direction as she mirrored her confused expression.

"Um," she suddenly recognized the child as one of the young girls that dined with Ignatius' family, maybe one of Locke's daughters, "Do you need something?"

"No," Kailey just stared at Aleisha, copying her every movement as she did. Aleisha was stuck; she had no idea how to respond to this child sitting on her bed.

"Aleisha," she sighed in relief when she heard Conner outside her room, he would know what to do with her new little friend. She rolled her eyes when she heard Kailey's echoing sigh.

"Can you see what Conner wants while I get dressed?"

"Ok," Kailey jumped up eagerly and bounced over to the exit, disappearing into the wall of ivy. Aleisha crawled out of bed and headed over to her small wardrobe and opened it up, she chose a brown dress identical to the one she had worn the day before, refusing to wear the color so often associated with Darksouls.

No sooner had she finished straightening the dress over her tall form, than she saw Conner move the curtain aside and enter her room; she wondered momentarily if he had been watching her, but dismissed the idea as quickly as it came. Conner was too decent a man to do that. "Where's Kailey?"

He smiled and shook his head, like he was laughing at a private joke. "I sent her to her father. She is so like her Uncle Garret, I hope she didn't bother you too much," he came farther into her room and picked up the dress she had left on the floor the night before, raising an eyebrow at her as if to ask why she would leave it there. "Garret followed me everywhere last time I was here; it would not surprise me if you have gotten yourself a shadow in his niece." He tossed the dress onto the foot of her bed and leaned gently on the edge of her desk.

"She mostly just startled me, I wasn't expecting any company," and that included him. He had disappeared after dinner last night, and she hadn't seen him since.

"I spoke to Byron and the others last night," he reached to scratch his neck, as he often did when thinking, "about you not wanting to be trained by Briganti. Since you now know about my power, we all agreed that it would be better for you to learn from me than one of the dragons, since I relate to magic the same way you do."

He seemed to be watching for her response, trying to decipher what she thought of the idea. She was just relieved that she didn't have to learn from Briganti; she didn't trust her shady Dictator and she had a sneaking suspicion that, under his training, she would find it too easy to become what everybody expected of a Darksoul.

She wanted to be different. She would not use her gift of hearing against her friends, and she would not use her magic to harm or manipulate as her father had. She believed that, with Conner's training and the guidance of the True God, she could be the first Darksoul to escape corruption.

After watching her process his words, Conner offered her a half smile and stood to leave. "I will need to inform Briganti that I will be training you, but we should be able to begin after breakfast."

He had just reached the doorway and was about to leave as she turned to him suddenly, "Conner," she watched as he looked back at her, confusion playing in his dark eyes, "I think it would be more appropriate for me to tell him." She didn't want to take the chance that Briganti would share what he told her yesterday, but Conner seemed to think she was just being polite because he smiled a little and nodded before turning again to leave.

Aleisha began pacing her room again, trying to find the best course of action. She knew that she would have to tell Briganti before breakfast, but she wasn't sure how to convince him not to tell anyone who she really was. She remembered then that some people at least suspected already. She really hoped that Locke would keep his suspicions to himself, but Conner had made it sound like having a Darksoul around was a great advantage to the people of Puko, and she somehow doubted that he would remain silent if he thought revealing her secret would cause her companions to leave her behind. She would not allow a foolish young boy to steal her newfound freedom by keeping her here through some mad manipulation. Knowing what she had to do; Aleisha straightened her back and headed out of her room and down the staircase.

When she reached Briganti's room, she entered without knocking, by this time having decided that it was not considered necessary in this odd little village. Inside, she saw the Dictator sitting at his desk, reading one of the books from the shelf she had seen the day before. "Good morning Aleisha," he didn't even look up when he addressed her, "did you sleep well?"

Guessing what he expected and desired to hear, she decided to answer in the most frustrating way possible, "Yes, I did. Thank you," she almost sang the words as she added a bit too much enthusiasm to her charmed voice, "After a long talk with Conner, I decided that I shouldn't have gotten so angry yesterday, so I wanted to apologize for my momentary lapse in judgment." She could tell by the way he placed the book down with forced grace and turned to her with an upset look on his face that this was not the answer he had been wanting. He had wanted her to be angry still. He had wanted her to let the anger take root and begin to grow an indestructible tree of bitterness and hatred. She took pleasure in the fact that she had not given him the satisfaction.

"You aren't upset about what you learned yesterday?" He stood up and stepped toward her, "Did you even ask Byron to show Tallen to you?"

"Oh, no; I couldn't bring myself to put such a caring soul through having to see his mate's murderer again," she pouted slightly and shook her head, trying to show him what a gentle girl she was and how impossible it would be for her to 'harness the evil inside her' as he had put it, "I spoke to Snarf instead, he showed me the exact image of my father." Again, she pouted.

"So, you see that I spoke the truth," he smiled cruelly as he said it, thinking that he could cause her to become angry again.

"Of course, why do you think I'm so ashamed of becoming angry with you?" She could see that she had confused him, so she continued, "All you did was reveal my father's true nature to me. I had been wondering if he was a Darksoul for a little while and you answered that question," she tilted her head slightly, giving the impression that she was a harmless little girl. She had often used her innocent eyes to manipulate Cedrick's opinion of her, causing him to think that she was too young and too naive to deceive him while all the time hiding from him, usually something like a scared young slave who was hiding from some punishment he had in store for them. She now used her gentle appearance to further anger the old man before her, "I can't even be mad at you for lying to me, since you did not," she ended and offered him a small smile. Pretending to become distracted by the bookshelf, she walked further into the room, hiding her face from his so that she could allow herself to return to a relaxed expression.

"But what of your father's bribe?" she could hear him step closer to her as he spoke, "Do you want to know what he offered me?"

"Not really," she turned to him and frowned, "I already know what a small amount he sold me for. I don't really care anymore how much I am or am not worth to my father." She had a sinking feeling that he was going to tell her anyway, so she turned her back to him so that he could not see the pain in her eyes when he revealed what her magic had been bought for; it was probably a much higher price than what Cedrick had paid for her.

"He offered your mother," Aleisha heard her pained gasp as he spoke the words, "It seems that, much like my late wife Zipporah, your mother does not age. Tallen thought that this small fact would make her a perfect slave, or a perfect wife if that was what I desired." Aleisha felt sick as the words continued to pour from his mouth.

"I did not accept of course," she could hear the tone in his voice change; he was done trying to make her hate her father, thinking that he had already succeeded in that, and was now trying to cause her to admire him. "I will not be bribed by the man who murdered my chosen babe. Nothing matters to me more than my babe."

She spun toward him then, holding her head high to show him that he did not control her, "Then why did you choose me, if not to accept his bribe?"

She saw him sneer as he answered her, showing the sinister look in his eyes that she had already noticed a few times. "To hurt him," at her confused expression, he smiled, "I knew that when I did not accept his wife that he would believe that I would choose another for the Darksoul power. I also knew that he would try to trade you away for something better when the opportunity arose, just as he did with your mother. I decided that I would choose you, so that when he met you again, he would see that he had sold the thing that he had desired most." Briganti sat in his chair and picked up the book he had been reading earlier, trying to look nonchalant, "I was the one who sent Cedrick to buy you from your father, promising him great reward for keeping you until I was ready to take you. I wanted Tallen to see that he had had exactly what he wanted and sold it for almost nothing." He clapped his hands and laughed once, "Can you just see his face when he realizes what a fool he was?"

Aleisha had to breathe deeply to steady the angry shivers that spread through her body. She resented being used as a chess piece, a pawn in Briganti's plan for revenge. "I have asked Conner to train me to control my magic." She flinched as she heard the book slam onto the wooden desk and she saw Briganti fly out of his chair with inhuman speed. Before she had time to react, he had his hand around her throat.

"What did you say?" he spoke in slow, hushed tones as he spat the words through his teeth.

"Conner will continue my training, I don't need you," she also spoke quietly, though she did so with a false calm that was only meant to frustrate him farther.

Briganti tightened his hold on her neck, staring into her eyes with a murderous look on his face, "You will want to rethink your plan, my dear. Conner will likely refuse to have anything to do with you when he learns what you are," he closed his fist tighter and leaned close to her face, "remember that he hates Darksouls like they were Ban himself."

Aleisha shivered, hearing the threat in his voice, and tried to calm her racing heart. "Tell me something, Briganti; do you know what happens when a Dictator dies? Is his chosen babe freed from the magic he was given?" she saw the torch above Briganti's desk lift from its holder. The flame it carried grew stronger as it moved closer to the pair, "If you even suggest my lineage to Conner or his dragons, we will discover the answer to that question together." He growled but loosened his hand from her throat. She breathed in a slow breath, trying to calm the anger that was making it difficult to control the torch, which was now completely engulfed in flame and hovering right next to the Dictator's head. Through the arrogant mask he was keeping carefully in place, she could see fear building in his eyes; he had never had his own babe threaten him before and knew that if she decided to kill him, no one would stop her. What he didn't know, and Aleisha was grateful for his ignorance, was that Conner was right; she did not have the evil in her that most Darksouls possessed and so would never kill him.

Taking one more calming breath, she moved around Briganti and stepped through his ivy curtain, letting the torch drop behind her. She heard his terrified yelp as it hit the ground, catching any loose paper and dried twigs on fire. She stood outside of his room for a few moments, letting the fire spread so that he would know that she could kill him if she wanted. When she saw the ivy curtain completely engulfed in flame and heard him scream in a voice that could only mean that he, too, had been touched, she extinguished the fire, stopping it before it could catch the live wood of the tree and letting Briganti know that she was not the monster he wanted her to be. As soon as the inferno ceased, and the ivy fell to the floor in a pile of ash, she turned away from the room and started down the stairs, confident that she had silenced the Dictator for a little while at least.

As Aleisha stormed out of the tree, she collided with Conner's wide chest. His hands moved instantly to her upper arms, steadying her as he gently pushed her back an arm's length away from him. "Did you have to set his room on fire?" She wasn't sure at first how he knew she had done that, but then she noticed several people rushing about, panicking at the sight of the smoke that had begun pouring into the clearing.

"It made a point," he raised an eyebrow at her, so she elaborated; "When I told him that you would continue my training, he threatened me. I had to show him that I would not be threatened."

Conner let out a frustrated sigh, "You gave him the reaction he wanted Aleisha; you need to learn how not to respond in such anger." He took her hand and led her back into the tree and directed her up the stairs. "The Creator says, 'be angry and do not sin,' this means that getting angry is fine. You can't control your immediate emotional response, but you must control your reactions to those emotions. Allowing your anger to direct your actions will always end badly and the more often you allow yourself to respond wrongly to your anger, the harder it will become for you to change that habit."

"So, what should I have done, then?" She pulled her hand from his, stopping on the path, and folding her arms. "I can't let him blackmail me into doing whatever he pleases; I had to show strength." She could hear Briganti still screaming as some flames continued burning in his room.

106

"You're confusing strength with violence, Aleisha. You can let him know that he doesn't own you without threatening his life; you're not his chosen babe, he has no claim to you." He had no idea how wrong he was. He did have claim to her, and she didn't see any way to be free of him without some show of force. He directed a young man away from the entrance of Briganti's room, and turned toward the smoke, staring at it until it began to dissipate.

"So, what should I have done then?"

"You could have shown him you were not afraid of his threats." He smiled gently as he continued, the ivy curtain now beginning to reform, as Fortuna gently pushed past them to enter his room, "You can trust me and my brothers to protect you from him, no matter what he is threatening to do to you. You could have just walked away, told me about his threat, and let him do what he will." Sure, except that he was threatening to destroy their friendship; Conner couldn't save her from that. "Come with me, Aleisha," he held out his hand to her, the room now fully restored, and its resident being tended to. "They are waiting for us. We can discuss this more later if you like." With Briganti's pathetic cries fading behind them, he guided her back out of the tree and onto the same path that Briganti had brought her down only the evening before.

Chapter 11

He led her to the same open area that Briganti had brought her to the day before. Snarf had prepared breakfast for them, and she had been grateful for the chance to eat alone with the group, as she didn't enjoy eating with Briganti and Ignatius' sons. As she stuffed her last bite in her mouth, Dagmar spoke, *"This is the same area Briganti used to train you?"* She nodded slightly; enough to be seen if he was looking, but not so much as to be obvious if that question was not meant for her, *"Do you know the significance of this hill? I'm sure you sense the power that it holds."* She shook her head slowly, uneasy for the pleasant manner with which he addressed her. *"This is the hill on which the first Darksoul died; he was hunted by the warrior chosen by Philimina so many years ago to end the war between the three nations of Elbot. After the warrior caught up with the Darksoul, there was a great battle. Many trees were burnt down, even as far as the entire village of Puko, which was not yet in existence. The magic battle that they fought lasted many days, but the great Dragonsoul eventually prevailed; summoning all of his power to destroy the abomination; he nearly killed himself and left this area bare of plant life."* He turned in a circle, sweeping his tail behind him dramatically, *"As you can see, the effect of that battle is still evident today."*

"So, why is that significant to my being here?" She could see Dagmar's countenance change to a more familiar expression. He hopped down from his rock and almost slithered toward her.

"It seems an appropriate place to destroy the dark soul inside of you," she did not miss the slight pause in his speech, just enough as to miss accusing her outright of being one of the evil creatures. He had no idea how accurate that would have been.

"If you are going to accuse me, don't dance around the words." She could feel every muscle in her body tense as she glared at him.

"Aleisha," Conner was standing beside her and placed a hand on her shoulder, "remember what I told you. Be angry, and do not sin." She hadn't even noticed that she had lifted a large rock and was prepared to hurl it at Dagmar. "Close your eyes and take a deep breath." She didn't need Conner to talk her through this. This was between her and Dagmar, and if he was going to be constantly accusing her of being evil, she had a right to defend herself. "Aleisha, close your eyes." Seeing Snarf's pleading expression, she relented. "Good, now focus on that rock. Feel the connection you have to it." She had no idea how to do that, she wasn't anywhere near the rock, she couldn't see, hear, or feel it. How was she supposed to establish a connection?

"Use your magic like your sixth sense, Aleisha," Snarf spoke after several minutes, *"You are trying to feel it physically when you need to feel it magically. You are holding it with your power, not your hand."* She tried to picture the rock in her mind, she imagined herself standing in an empty space, with only the rock, floating above the earth, with her in the image.

As she concentrated on giving the rock more detail in her mind, she could see a thin strand of pulsing mist between her and the rock. She tried to control the mist, pulling on it with her hands in her vision. Much to her delight, the rock moved slightly, *"Good,"* Snarf's voice entered the emptiness, bringing his form with it. He appeared to be made solely of the brilliant white mist, *"now you need to place it, gently, back where it was."*

"I can't see where that is; I can only see you and the rock," she looked around her. She was still surrounded with empty space.

"She's a quick study," Grezald's voice, followed by his form in the white mist, appeared several yards away.

"Try to remember your surroundings exactly, Aleisha. The more detail you add, the better you will be able to see." She tried to remember exactly where everybody was standing; she struggled slightly with Conner, as he had apparently moved away from her since she had closed her eyes. She then added the fire to her empty space, surprised to see that it had no white mist in it; perhaps only living beings gave off the mist. A squirrel ran across the clearing, knocking pebbles out of the way as he went. Again, no white mist, but she could almost feel the tiny creature breathing. *"Do you have it yet?"* she nodded, not entirely sure anymore if she was only nodding in her vision or not. *"Good, now return the rock to its resting place."* She reached out again to pull on the mist, *"Use your mind, Aleisha. The magic is a part of you, just as your arms and legs are a part of you."* She tried again, this time willing it to move the boulder, ever so slowly, to the crater in the ground where it had previously resided.

As soon as she let go of the rock, she opened her eyes, "Good job, Aleisha," Conner smiled at her, grasping her shoulder with pride, "I'm impressed you figured out so

110

quickly how to do that; you have incredible instincts. Use that to train on your own in your spare time." She only nodded, exhausted from the experience, and feeling slightly silly for allowing Dagmar to elicit such a reaction from her. She knew that he was just extremely protective of his family; he would not trust her easily simply for not knowing her. Adding the fact that he was right about her, that she really was a Darksoul, she didn't have any right to be angry with him.

Aleisha lay in her bed staring at the ceiling. She had been training almost nonstop for two weeks, and she was exhausted. Every day, Conner would have her work in her strange vision world for several hours, just standing and watching how the world moved around her. He said that if she got good enough at it, she would be able to sense the world around her with the same intensity any time she needed to; much as she had the first time she stormed away from her training with Briganti. This, as he had explained after she had accidentally walked in on him getting dressed a few days ago, was how he knew when it was safe to enter her room unannounced.

She was getting a lot better at controlling her power when she was calm and could think about what she wanted to do, but today, she had become frustrated with Conner as he tried to explain, again, how to make images with the dirt. She had often succeeded in doing so, but only while she was unaware of it, she didn't seem to be able to control that particular ability, and so she had gotten mad. She'd almost killed him when a small pile of debris exploded with her frustration. He was thrown back with the force as dozens of rocks slammed

111

into him. The last she had seen of him, he was lying on his back, bleeding from several wounds, including a large gash on his head. Snarf had grabbed her at that point and carried her back to the village as the others tended to Conner.

She rolled to her side to stare at her door, hoping to see Conner walking past her room. She hoped that he would be ok. She knew that his wounds would heal with Byron's help, but she was sure that he would be angry with her for hurting him so badly.

She heard some shuffling outside of her room and wondered if that could be Conner; he was usually almost silent, but he might still have a headache even after being healed, so it was possible that he would be slightly less graceful. When the footsteps ended outside of her room, she sat up to greet her visitor, not entirely surprised, or thrilled, to see Kailey. The little girl stopped momentarily at the door before bounding inside like an excited puppy. Aleisha couldn't help but be slightly suspicious of the girl, as she was Locke's daughter, but she only seemed to be fascinated with Aleisha. "The tall man came staggering into the Common Tree a few minutes ago. I think he got hit in the head because he was squinting like he had a bad headache." Even as she delivered what should have been sober news, she smiled just like her uncle would have if he had given the report.

"Thank you, Kailey, I was wondering if he was back yet," she tried to return the girl's smile, but she wasn't sure she succeeded. Kailey sat down on the bed next to her and smiled up at her, tapping her feet together a few inches above the floor.

"Are you and him married?"

"Why would you ask that?" Aleisha tilted her head to give her an amused look; she wondered why everybody was so worried with Conner's relationship status.

"You always leave together, and he is protective of you like Pater is of Mater," her eyes were wide and innocent, like she didn't realize how odd her logic was.

"No, we're not married. He is training me how to control my magic," Kailey obviously didn't understand what she meant, so she tried again, "Like when your mater was teaching you to cook, he is teaching me the same way." She nodded, seeming to accept her explanation. Aleisha watched as her young companion looked about her room, taking in all that surrounded her.

"You should have a picture," she suddenly hopped up and strode over to Aleisha's desk, opening up the drawer and retrieving a piece of parchment. "I will paint you a picture to hang on your wall so that it is not so boring." As the girl sat on the chair and instantly became lost in her work, Aleisha stood up and headed to her doorway, planning to take a walk while Kailey worked.

A month ago, she would have found it odd, such a young girl talking of painting as if it were a common activity, but she had since gotten used to the wealth of this town. The residents didn't even seem to realize how truly wealthy they were.

As she stepped out of her room, she looked across the tree to Conner's room, wondering if he was back yet; she wanted to apologize for hurting him. She closed her eyes and focused on the tree around her, trying to summon the connected feeling she used when controlling her magic. When she didn't sense any movement in his room, she decided to head down the staircase; hoping that by the time she reached the bottom and got back to her room, Kailey would be done with her drawing and could be persuaded to find her father and leave Aleisha with some privacy.

She was about halfway down the steps when she felt a presence in Briganti's quarters; she had managed to avoid him since their last encounter when she told him that Conner would continue her training, and she wasn't in the mood to see him now. She paused for a moment, trying to sense what he was doing so she could gauge whether or not she could sneak past him. Sensing him walking toward the door, she turned around and began walking back up the staircase, hoping that he wouldn't call to her when he saw her rushing away from him. "Aleisha," she hadn't even managed to ascend half a dozen steps before hearing him behind her.

She stopped and turned toward the old man, hoping that he couldn't see the exhaustion in her eyes, "What do you want?"

"I only wanted to know how your training was going," he climbed a few steps so that they were only a few feet apart, "I am still your Dictator and care deeply about your welfare. I want to see you succeed, but since I am not a part of your training, I can't see for myself how well you are doing."

"My training is none of your concern, and you are dull if you think that I believe you for a moment about caring for my wellbeing," she glared at the Dictator and breathed deeply, bringing her mind into focus so that she could see every individual gray hair in his beard.

"I didn't think that you would tell me, you do still seem upset about your father."

"I am not upset about my father, foolish old man," she spat at him, instantly remembering the phrase Conner would repeat every time they trained: be angry and do not sin. She would not attack Briganti, though she surely wanted to. She knew that if she tried to keep herself from harming him for his sake that he would be laying on the tree floor in seconds, but she knew the look of disappointment she would see in Snarf's eyes if she hurt the old man and so she would control herself for his sake rather than Briganti's. "I am upset because I do not like to be used as a pawn in your pathetic attempt to get revenge on my father."

Conner stepped into the dwelling then, distracting Aleisha from her conversation. He looked like he had a bad headache, but she didn't see any evidence that he was still bleeding, so she let out a small sigh of relief. Pushing past Briganti, she hurried down the remainder of the stairs and ran over to him, stopping when she saw the look of compassion in his eyes. She had been expecting anger, frustration, or even hurt, but never had she thought that he would have felt sorry for her. "Are you alright?" he asked. Aleisha felt her mouth drop open slightly; he was the one with blood all over his shirt, and he was asking if she was alright? "I know you feel awful about what happened."

"I could have killed you."

"No, you couldn't have," Conner shook his head, smiling to reassure her, "Byron would have never let that happen." Aleisha felt Briganti walk up behind her.

"I take it training is not going as well as you had hoped," the Dictator stared pointedly at the drying blood on Conner's shirt, "Perhaps you should rethink my offer to continue your training, Aleisha, before someone gets killed." By the neutral look on Conner's face, she was willing to bet that he missed the threat in Briganti's voice.

"Give me a few more weeks with her, Briganti. I have an idea that might help her."

"Very well," the old man let out an exaggerated sigh, "I just think that it would be best for a young magic user to learn from a Dictator."

"It would be best for her to learn from her Dictator, but, since we don't know who that is, I think we should let her decide who should train her." Aleisha bit her lip and glanced nervously at Briganti, wondering if he feared her enough to keep his mouth shut. She noticed that the back of his neck was wrapped in cloth and he reached up to massage the area around it, as if remembering the fire that she had set in his room to give him that wound. He would remain silent for as long as she needed him to; he valued his life too much to defy her.

"Very well, but I would still suggest that she stop by my quarters later so that I may show her some of my books that may be helpful," he looked at her then, demanding rather than asking that she comply. He knew that she feared the information he threatened to use against her as much as he feared the force she threatened against him. He knew that he would see her in his room if he demanded it, because she would do anything to keep her friends from finding out what she was. So, when he smiled at her with the same devious look she had seen in his eyes so many times, she nodded, letting him know that he had won this battle.

Chapter 12

Aleisha entered her room and collapsed onto her bed, frustrated from her encounter with Briganti. She had wanted to ask what Conner's idea was to help her train but thought better of it because Briganti had been there; she was sure she would find out tomorrow anyway. A loud squeak and gentle shaking of her bed drew her out of her thoughts and reminded her that she had left her visitor alone in her room for almost an hour. Kailey sat next to her and petted her hair, smoothing it over the pillow she was laying on, "I finished designing your picture," the girl's sweet smile was not in place as it usually was, and Aleisha wondered if she could sense the turmoil she was experiencing.

Aleisha sat up, trying to give the girl a convincing smile, "May I see it?" Kailey jumped up and hurried over to the desk, grabbed the parchment, and rushed back to Aleisha to hold it up proudly. The picture was of a large dragon with a girl on its back, it appeared to be flying over either a forest or a large fire; she wasn't sure which. "That is lovely Kailey; you did a very good job." She offered her a genuine smile this time, impressed by the girl's artistic ability. The little girl's broad smile widened even further at the compliment and she ran back to the desk.

"I'll start painting it after dinner tonight and, when I'm finished, I'll have Pater help me make a frame for it. Then you can see it all the time and you can smile and remember that I gave it to you," she was talking so quickly as she rummaged through the drawer that

118

Aleisha could barely understand a thing she was saying, but before she could tell her to slow down, she had slammed the drawer shut, apparently giving up on finding what she needed, and ran out the doorway.

Aleisha stared after the girl for a moment, half wondering if she would come back, or if she could go to dinner without worrying about Kailey being alone in her room again. Before she had a moment to decide, Conner stepped into her room, "I thought you might want to speak to me without the threat of Briganti's interruption," he stood just inside the doorway, not quite looking confident as to whether he was welcome to enter.

"I didn't mean to hurt you," she blurted out what she had been trying to say when he first arrived in the tree, but Conner only smiled in response. He seemed unconcerned with the matter entirely.

"I know that you do not mean what you do with your magic when you are upset." He offered her a reassuring smile, trying to calm the guilt that she felt so heavily weighing on her, "I've seen the way you react to what you have done, and I see that it only frustrates you further." He rubbed the back of his neck and stared at the floor for a moment, "It's as if your magic is activated by your emotions, it's like it's pure feeling come to life; anger becomes violence, nostalgia becomes pictures, who knows what joy or fear could create?" His eyes seemed to widen as he spoke, and his speech sped up as he continued, obviously excited about the prospect of what he had just discovered. "I think that it's probably because you learned about your magic so late."

"But why would that make a difference?" She couldn't see why her age would have anything to do with how her magic manifested itself, "Shouldn't my magic be the same as everybody else's? It's not like I was given a different kind of magic."

Conner shook his head and stood up. He began pacing excitedly across her floor, any remainder of a headache forgotten, "Remember that I told you the Creator bound our magic to our emotions; the two have always been connected. Most Dictators, when they choose a babe, become invested in the child's life. Training begins when the child is very young, and magic is taught like speaking, walking, or manners are taught; it is just another part of life and very important to the child's development." Aleisha still didn't see the connection, so he continued, "What do you think would happen if a child were never taught the value of tact? They would find it very difficult as an adult to separate their natural inclination to speak every word that enters their mind from the need to censor what they say to keep from hurting the people around them. The same seems to be true of your magic in that you need to learn how to separate your magical inclination to act on every emotion from the need to guard all that you do.

"If we can help you separate the two sides of your magic, the emotion and the action, then we should be able to change your trigger from your emotion to your will." As he continued talking excitedly, waving his hands enthusiastically as he rambled about properties of magic she had never heard of before, she could only watch him in amazement.

Conner suddenly stopped to stare at her, his eyes still wide as he gazed at her in wonder. "No matter what the outcome, Aleisha, you will be a very powerful and unique magic user." With that, he stood up and exited the room.

Aleisha stared after him for a few moments, frustrated by her inability to understand him; he often held an intelligent conversation with her for a few minutes before seeming to become distracted by some unknown force and hurrying away from her. She wondered if he was somehow uncomfortable being alone with her, as he seemed to become less comfortable and more easily distracted when no one else was in the room.

Shaking her head to clear her thoughts, she left her room and began, again, descending the steps to join the others that would be eating dinner at this time. As she took her foot off of the last step, she heard a loud crash from right outside the tree, followed by loud squeals of laughter. Curious about what she might find outside, she headed toward the commotion. Kailey sat in a puddle of brown sludge with a bowl sitting, upside down, on her head and more of the brown goo dripping down her face. Another girl, who she recognized as Garret's oldest daughter, stood just to the side of her, laughing. Kailey was a sweet girl and would often try to help people carry some of the dishes to dinner, but she was also a very clumsy girl and would often end up on the ground, covered in whatever she was trying to carry.

Aleisha tried to suppress her laughter as she bent to look the girl in her eyes. Taking the bowl off of her head, she began wiping some of the gravy from her face, "Where were you two headed with this?"

"Uncle Locke wanted some gravy for his potatoes and bread, so Kailey and I offered to get him some," the older girl answered her, "but Kailey decided that she should wear it instead, so now we don't have any to bring to Uncle Locke." She ended with another girlish laugh, covering her mouth with her hand to hide her giggles, as Kailey threw some of the sticky mess in her direction.

Aleisha laughed at the girls' antics as she stood and offered her hand to Kailey. Helping the girl up, she turned her toward the creek that flowed near the clearing, "Let's get you cleaned up, then we'll look for more gravy to bring to your father."

"Agabeth can get Pater some gravy; she doesn't need to clean up," Kailey smiled up at Aleisha as she walked quickly to the creek.

Before Aleisha could chase after her, Agabeth grabbed her by the arm. "My uncle doesn't like you." The sweet, laughing girl of just a moment ago had disappeared to be replaced by a much more serious, malicious looking child.

"I know he doesn't," She wasn't sure why Agabeth felt the need to bring this up, but if she was anything like her uncle, as Kailey was like hers, then she wasn't going to enjoy this conversation.

"He doesn't like you being trained by the dragon boy instead of your Dictator." The tone with which she spoke was suspiciously close to threatening as she glared cruelly at Aleisha.

"Did your uncle ask you to tell me this?"

"I think it is only fair that you know that your continued relationship with the dragons and their pet would be to your detriment. None of us want to see anything happen to Briganti's chosen babe, and Uncle Locke fears that you may end up dead if you continue to train with them." That was most definitely a threat. Aleisha was tired of being threatened. This ten-year-old was not going to get away with such disrespectful and foolish behavior. As Aleisha felt the all too familiar sensation of her magic rising to defend her, she remembered Conner's gentle words, *be angry and do not sin.* Suddenly feeling sick over whatever she was just about to do to the child, she turned, pulling her arm away from the girl, and walked away before she could change her mind.

Meals were always eaten in the Common Tree, with nearly everybody in Puko present and enjoying loud fellowship and tasty food. The lack of privacy while eating had been difficult for Aleisha to get accustomed to, but she had come to appreciate the fellowship, as this was one of the few times she would see anybody that didn't live in her tree.

As she entered, she quickly scanned the room for Conner and the dragons, as she had eaten every meal with them since arriving, but when she sensed eyes on her from across the room, she headed toward Locke, fully prepared to unleash the anger she had held back from his niece on him.

"Has the honored Darksoul finally chosen to accept her place with the leaders of Puko?" She had to restrain herself from spitting in his face when he spoke, knowing fully that she had no intention of joining them.

"So, I am honored now? I must admit I did not feel honored when Agabeth relayed your threat."

Locke raised one eyebrow as she spoke, "I'm sorry, I'm afraid I have no idea what threat you are talking about."

"You fear that I might end up dead if I continue to train with Conner and the dragons? What would you call that if not a threat?"

"Justified concern," Locke stepped closer to her so that their faces were only a few inches apart, a movement that would have intimidated her only a few months ago. "Don't you worry what they would do to you if they found out who you really are? I haven't told them because I fear for your life, not because I don't think it would deter them from training you." He squinted at her, trying to make her see his side, "Do you think you can hide your true nature from them forever? Don't think that I want them to find you out, as I said, I fear for you, but I don't think that you can hide yourself from five dragons and a Dragonsoul indefinitely."

Aleisha had no immediate response to this, as he sounded disturbingly reasonable in his argument. She knew exactly what they would do to her if they knew what she was, at least if they fulfilled their threat of a Darksoul barbeque. "I can see that you know what I say to be true, so why do you continue to stay with them; to lie to them?"

"If I were to have Briganti train me, I would be telling Conner that I am what you say I am. If you fear for my life so much, why do you want me to have him train me so badly? Could it be because you know that he would do everything in his power to make me like every

124

Darksoul before me? Could it be because you want a powerful magic user blessing your little village as my predecessor did?" Aleisha felt the fire under a nearby stewpot heat up as she spoke. Breathing deeply, she tried her best to calm the flames as she stared into Locke's eyes. "I refuse to believe that you care at all what happens to me. As your niece said, you don't like me. You only care about the profit of yourself and your pathetic village." On finishing, she felt a quick sting as he slapped her.

Every flame within twenty feet of them suddenly exploded into an inferno, and then ceased altogether as she tried to bring them under control. Aleisha glared at Locke, who suddenly did not look very sure of himself. The fiery display had attracted the entire room's attention, and everybody held their breaths as they waited to see what the powerful young magic user would do. Aleisha sensed Conner looking at her, sensed him analyzing her reaction to see if she could control herself. Every pile of wood that had ceased its burning began to ice as she continued to stare at the man in front of her, who had backed up several feet when his fire pit had exploded only a few feet from him.

She could feel every eye on her as she continued to cool the temperature in the room, feeling the ice spread from the wood to the grass surrounding it. She tried to remember the words that Snarf had said to her countless times since they began training, *"Be angry, and do not sin."* She repeated this simple phrase more than a dozen times to herself before finally sensing the ice recede from its borders and small flames restart in the chilled pits. "You will keep yourself and your family away from both me and my friends. Do you understand?" She could see in his eyes that he feared her enough to obey. She did not want to be feared, as that was the legacy of Darksouls, but in this instance, she supposed it would have to do.

She turned from him and headed toward Conner, who wore a small smile as she approached. "Well done Aleisha," She had not expected that response, she had nearly set the whole tree aflame, then overcorrected and almost froze everyone inside. "You stopped yourself without needing any of us to interfere." He smiled at her when he said this, letting her know that he was proud of her for her display of control, no matter how small. She had finally shown the first sign of improvement.

Chapter 13

After five awkward minutes of trying to ignore the suspicious and fearful looks being directed at her by the diners, Aleisha grabbed a large piece of bread and a few chunks of meat. Piling them together in one of her hands, she stood and headed to the exit. Sensing Conner only a few steps behind her, she moved quickly toward the Karr River to enjoy her meal by the cold tributary that flowed near the clearing.

As she broke through the trees that separated the village from the water's edge, she slowed her pace as an invitation for Conner to catch up with her. His large form appeared next to her as they walked silently the rest of the distance to the stream, and he still did not speak when they sat down and Aleisha dropped her feet into the icy water. She tore her bread into two pieces and began ripping into the larger one with her teeth, staring across the water and wondering what her companion was thinking. She knew he would speak when he was ready, but she wished that he didn't so often take so long to become ready.

Almost as soon as she swallowed the last bite of her dinner, she felt Conner shift next to her, repositioning his long legs so that they were folded under him. "Can you make the water dance?"

"What?" why would he ask that? He knew that she couldn't. She had tried so many times already and had only succeeded in embarrassing herself.

"I want to see you control the water. Do you think you can do it?" She nodded, not because she thought she could, but because she understood why he was asking, she needed a distraction from her frustrated musings.

She let out a deep breath to focus her concentration as she stared at the river and wondered how one goes about controlling something like water. She tried to remember what she felt when she had influenced things in the past, but it was hard to separate the emotions she felt from the sensations. After staring at the water moving slowly over the rocks in the stream for a few minutes, she heard Conner chuckling beside her. "Are you going to begin?"

"What do you think I've been trying to do?"

He squinted at her then, as if analyzing her, "I'm not sure. Have you even decided exactly what you are trying to do?" he stood up and stretched his back, nodding to the water, "If you just tell it to dance, like I suggested, it will never do anything. You need to take control of it like you do with flames. You need to give it specific instructions," the water suddenly shot out of the stream, creating a pillar in front of Aleisha, "like that. Now you try."

Aleisha stood and moved next to Conner, hoping that somehow being closer to him could help her understand how he had controlled it. As she focused on the water near the grass she had been sitting on, she imagined that she was becoming fluid like the substance she was trying to control. She tried to imagine how she would move if she had no form and moved her arms slowly toward the sky as she tried to convince the water that it was her new body. To her great delight, a small wave formed on the surface of the stream.

Smiling now, she closed her eyes and imagined herself flowing over the rocks as the stream. After a few moments of concentration, she could almost feel the texture of the smooth rocks at the bottom of the stream slowly becoming rougher as they peaked out of the top of the water. As soon as she could feel herself flowing freely, completely detached from her body, she stopped moving. She felt the rocks underneath her, stopping her from seeping into the ground below; she even felt the few small fish, formerly riding the current to their destination, stop in confusion as their free ride ceased and they were forced to continue their journey by their own power.

Opening her eyes, she saw the stream as she had seen it a moment ago. Every detail was exactly as she remembered it, but by some odd phenomenon, she was also seeing herself through the water, as if she was the stream. She could see no definite shapes at first as everything was distorted by the refraction of light through the water, but as she focused, she could see herself clearly. Conner stood less than a foot away from her, looking at her expectantly as he waited for her to complete her task. He did not know that she had already succeeded; the water obeyed her perfectly.

She saw herself begin to smile as she stared, through the water, at herself and her teacher. At the same time, she saw the stream begin to flow in gentle circles as she began pulling herself together to create a tangible form as Conner had been expecting. As the form of a woman began materializing out of the water, she saw Conner smile and nod, satisfied that she had succeeded. "Who is she?" A woman now stood in the water before them. She was several inches shorter than Aleisha and quite a bit wider from head to foot as well. Her short hair fell just to her shoulders and her eyes held the expression of a woman who had been betrayed many times.

"My mother."

Aleisha and Conner spent several more hours by the water, and Conner showed her how to connect to the water without having to give her consciousness to it, as she had done in order to create her mother. She was amazed how easily she controlled it now that she had succeeded once. "You learn quickly, Aleisha." She was in the process of building her old cell room out of the dirt when Conner's voice broke through her concentration, sending the dirt falling to the ground. Smiling, he added, "But you need to learn how to stay focused; you'll rarely have the luxury of working in complete silence."

She was just opening her mouth to reply when a large form landed on the other side of the stream. *"Greetings,"* Snarf lowered his head to the water and took a long drink of the cool liquid. Aleisha was suddenly glad that she was no longer connected to the stream. *"How is training going?"*

"She is learning even faster than I had hoped. You were right about her." Conner smiled again as he gave a favorable report of his student.

"I knew she would be a good student; I was only worried about her teacher." Aleisha laughed at this as Conner shot the dragon a teasing glare.

"Maybe you should have offered to teach her then."

"You know very well that that would never have worked, I'm an awful teacher." Snarf shook his head as he sat down, settling in for a long rest.

130

"You're right. You're almost as bad a teacher as you are a student. It is definitely better that I train her." A large amount of water suddenly shot out of the stream, spraying Conner squarely in the face. Grinning, he raised his arms high, sending the entire stream flying toward the dragon. The ensuing minutes were filled with much laughter as dragon and humans all sprayed, splashed, and smacked each other with the water of the ice-cold stream.

Aleisha lifted a small fish out of the water to throw at Conner, but as soon as she released the creature, he ducked, sending the fish flying behind him and directly into the face of her Dictator. Hearing the sound of the wet fish colliding with skin, Conner turned toward Briganti. "Good evening," the old man nodded respectfully to Conner before removing the wiggling creature from his long beard and stepping toward Aleisha. "I have something in my study that I believe you will want to see, Aleisha," raising an eyebrow as he inspected his fish, he added, "as soon as you're done horsing about with your friends." With that, he turned and disappeared back into the trees, tossing the fish to the side as he walked.

"What was that about?" Conner stared after the old man, looking mildly offended.

"I don't know, and I don't want to." Aleisha sat on a nearby rock, frustrated by the old man's sudden appearance.

"I believe you should probably see what he wants to show you." Snarf spoke in a patient and calming voice; he knew that Briganti's presence upset her. *"It may be something important."*

"I don't care how important he thinks it is, I'm done listening to his taunting and lies. I won't be dragged into another fight with that man."

"Good," Conner stepped closer to her and sat on the only dry spot on the bank, "you should refuse to get into an argument with him. Especially because you know that that is exactly what he desires, but do you think that you can avoid him altogether? He will continue to harass you until you settle whatever dispute is going on between you."

"It cannot be settled without argument," she stood from her seat and began pacing in front of the stream, intensely aware of the two sets of eyes constantly watching her. "He will not leave me alone until I either give him what he wants, which I will never do, or leave."

"Are you sure there is no third option?"

"Quite sure, he only wants one thing from me and it is not to let him train me." She considered telling them of his plan to use her against her father but thought better of it because she did not want them knowing that he was her Dictator.

"Then I suggest you go and see him immediately," Conner raised his hand to stop her protest when she spun toward him, "See what he wants to show you because, as Snarf said, it could very well be important, and then tell him that we will be leaving in the morning. I see no reason to stay if it will gain you nothing, especially with the way my brothers and I have been treated during this visit."

"I agree wholeheartedly." Aleisha thought that the dragon seemed a little too excited by the idea of leaving,

but that could just be because it was Snarf and he could be over-excited about anything.

"So do I," she let a faint smile touch her lips at the thought of finally being free from the only people who could turn Conner and the dragons against her. Breathing a deep, fortifying breath, she looked to Conner for a final nod of encouragement and headed after Briganti.

Chapter 14

When Aleisha stepped into Briganti's room, she could see in his eyes that he hadn't expected her so soon. "You certainly didn't waste any time."

"We decided that I should see whatever it is you have to show me as soon as possible. Snarf and Conner seem to think that it's important."

"It is," Briganti moved to his book shelf and started moving books around; she was slightly surprised that none of the books showed signs of having been in a fire, but she supposed that Conner had restored them when he restored the rest of the room. "I wanted to give you your cloak."

"What do you mean 'my cloak'?" Briganti continued rearranging items on his book shelf until they were lined up in order by thickness of the binding. Aleisha thought this an odd way to organize books, but he nodded in satisfaction and moved to his desk.

"Go ahead and browse if you like, I know how you love to read." It was true that Aleisha had taken every chance she could to read in Cedrick's small library, but she was bothered that the old man could know that. He had said something earlier about keeping an eye on her while in Cedrick's possession.

Stepping cautiously toward the shelves, she began reading the titles of several old, worn out books, many of which she had already read. Two books on the end of the row were different from the rest; however, as they looked newer and were in a language she was not familiar with, "What are these two?"

"They are a project of mine; I am trying to translate them so that they may be added to the Great Library in Might City. The taller one is called *Primal* and the thick one is *Four Dimensional*. I'm sorry to say that I haven't gotten very far on either one, though *Four Dimensional* seems to be some sort of magical travel story."

"How would that work?"

"I'm not quite sure yet. As I said, I haven't gotten very far yet, but they seem to be using an enchanted room which can change places almost instantly." Briganti seemed quite pleased that she had asked and appeared to be ready to dive into a full explanation of the subject, but as interesting and confusing as the idea sounded; Aleisha suddenly remembered why she was here.

"You said something about my cloak. I don't have a cloak."

"Of course you don't, that is because I have not yet given it to you," the old man pulled a large piece of cloth out of his desk drawer and held it up for her to examine. It was a dark gray cloak with long sleeves and an enormous hood which could easily hide one's face if worn up. It was a very dark shade of gray at the hood and gradually became darker as it neared the bottom, where it was so black that it seemed to suck the light out of the air around it, giving it the appearance of being made of smoke. It looked exactly like the one her father wore when murdering Lorahlie.

"You want to give me that?" she stepped back in horror. Anyone who saw her in this cloak would know immediately of her origin and her dark power. It was indeed an important thing that he offered her, but she refused to be seen wearing the mark of a Darksoul. "I will not accept that."

"You fail to understand its significance then," Briganti sneered as he held the cloak out to her, "This cloak is much more than a simple piece of cloth."

"I know exactly what its significance is; it is a sign to the whole world that I am a Darksoul. Did you really think that I would wear something that would admit that I am a detestable creature known for murdering helpless souls who get in my way? I would rather be burned at the stake for your crimes, than wear them as my own."

"As I said, you fail to understand the cloak's significance," he lowered the cloth before her face, but not much. "This physical symbol of who you are is indeed something to be worn with delicate understanding of what it represents, but it is only a physical replica of your true cloak, the one you will discover in time and will not be able to hide from your beloved friends once you do." The old man stepped closer to Aleisha and whispered threateningly, "When you transform into your true form, as all magic users do when using great amounts of power, you will be seen as wearing a cloak identical to the one in my hand, and you will not be able to disguise your true nature from those dragons any longer, or that foolish Dragonsoul whom you so admire." Having spit out the final word, Briganti shoved the cloak into Aleisha's arms and strode angrily out of the room.

Aleisha stood in the empty room for a few moments, shuddering at the implications of what her Dictator had just revealed. Her greatest fear was Conner and the dragons finding out about her nature, and she was now being told that that was inevitable. As she stared at the cloth in her hand, and contemplated her next actions, the deep blackness of the hem seemed to drain any light and warmth the room had seemed to hold the moment before. No cloth could have such an effect on its surroundings without the aid of some dark magic that consumed it, and she wanted none of that magic to accompany her on her journey. Dropping the cloak to the floor before Briganti's desk, she turned her back to the accursed symbol and fled the room.

In her room, Aleisha quickly filled a pack that Fortuna had made for her out of one of the potato sacks with her few possessions. After cramming her brown dress and her mother's map into the large pocket, she also added a canteen that Conner had given her and two candles. She hoped dearly that she could convince Conner to leave tonight instead of waiting for morning, because she didn't think that Briganti would let her leave without telling Conner what she was.

As she threw the strap over her shoulder and turned to exit, Conner stepped into her room, the look he gave her suggested that he had already guessed that she was planning on leaving early, "I hope you know that fleeing won't save you any trouble."

"How is that? He can't touch me if I'm gone?"

"Even a Dictator dedicated to his town is free to leave at any time, and even if he doesn't, whatever he is using against you is obviously an internal battle for you; it will follow you wherever you go."

"Maybe it will be an easier problem to solve without him constantly trying to illicit an emotional response. If

I can get away from him, I can think through this whole thing with a clear head."

"Aleisha," he sighed as he stepped further into her quarters and claimed the seat at her desk, "you know you can trust me and my brothers with whatever this is, right?"

Shaking her head, she walked slowly to the corner of the room, staring at the wall as if it could answer all of her questions, "I'm not used to having anyone but myself; I need some time before involving you. It may not even be anything worth the fuss, but with Briganti trying to stir up a fight, everything is just being blown out of proportion."

"Will you at least agree to wait until morning to leave? The people of Puko like to see their visitors off and I wouldn't like to offend them by denying them that."

She spun around then, shocked at his attitude toward them, "They have done nothing but insult you since we arrived, why do you care if you offend them?"

"I considered them friends once," Conner stood and approached the door, "Besides, I hate to repay evil for evil; there is no better way to start a war than that, and I am not a fan of unnecessary conflict."

"As long as you promise me we will leave as early as possible, I will try to be patient." His kindness continued to surprise her. He never ceased to consider the feelings of others, to place them above himself.

"Then I'll tell Briganti that we'll be leaving," as Aleisha opened her mouth to protest, Conner raised his hand to stop her, "I'm sure you would prefer to tell him even if only to keep me away from him and whatever conflict you two have going on, but I think it best if I handle this. You would only get into another argument with him, and I think we all want to avoid that."

Aleisha spent the remainder of the evening in her room, worrying about Conner's conversation with Briganti. What if Briganti told him why she was so desperate to leave? What if Conner hated her when he found out what she was? What if he abandoned her to remain in this town with no way out?

Frustrated and exhausted by her contemplations, Aleisha found sleep to be an unattainable necessity that night, as she tried, and failed, to rest. Her bed had never felt so uncomfortable as it did that night as she tossed and turned in anticipation and fear. By morning, she had long since given up on the idea of sleep and opted to walk to the dragons' quarters and climb the endless steps to Snarf's room to find better rest under the great creature's wings.

She walked silently up countless steps to the dragon's room and moved slowly to his side so as not to startle him as he slept, only to find that his eyes were open, and he was watching her with the concerned expression that a parent might give their child that they found sneaking out of their home at night. "I couldn't sleep."

"I guessed that," he raised one wing in a welcoming manner to invite her into his warmth, *"Why did it take you so long to come?"*

"I didn't want to trouble you," as she burrowed deeper into Snarf's furry wing, she added, "Did you see Conner after he spoke to Briganti last night?"

"Is that what is bothering you?" the dragon let out a huff that sounded a lot like a sigh, *"Conner mentioned*

that you were worried about what Briganti might say to him, but he said that he didn't think that there was anything we should be concerned about. He worries about you, Aleisha. We all do."

"I wouldn't say all."

"Even Dagmar takes it as a personal offence that Briganti has offended you so thoroughly that we would be fleeing the very people we used to call friends. He may not trust or like you personally, but when any one of us claims you as family, we all do."

Aleisha could hear Snarf continue to speak comforting words, but his voice faded into unintelligible garble as she passed out from complete exhaustion.

Aleisha woke to a sudden gust of cold air as Snarf lifted his wing slightly from her sleeping form. As she opened her eyes, she found Conner sitting next to Snarf, talking quietly about the next leg of their journey, "Because she obviously doesn't know how to read the map."

"I told you she couldn't be trusted." Dagmar voiced his usual response to anything said about her.

"That isn't what I was saying at all, you know that she is just learning about magic. If her mother enchanted it so that only her daughter could access it rather than so that only her daughter could read it, then it could simply be that she doesn't know how to use it. If that is the case, I think we should head to Fonishia. We can talk to Elam, he's always been good at solving such puzzles.

"Or we could head to Shiloh and seek out Philimina." Grizwald added, *"I'm sure he would be pleased to help."*

"We just got out of there," Conner practically shouted his response, obviously disliking the idea for more reasons than he let on.

"I have to agree with Conner this time. Visiting Philimina would gain us nothing." Grezald spoke in rare opposition to his twin.

"Maybe he can tell Aleisha what kind of magic user she is. That would certainly be something to gain." Grizwald countered.

Aleisha sat up then, hoping to reveal her consciousness and distract from the current direction of the conversation. "Mornin'," she smiled as Conner gave his usual greeting, "We were just discussing where we should go from here, any suggestions?"

Shaking her head, she finally admitted defeat. "You're right; I don't know how to read my mother's map. I'm sorry I didn't say anything; I didn't know how to admit that I had failed even before we started our journey."

"Just because you don't know how to read the map yet does not mean that we have failed at anything," When Byron spoke, he commanded the attention of everyone in the room, as he always did, *"We were discussing the best strategy to help you learn how to access the map; there are people who can help."*

"Conner mentioned a place called Fonishia, I've never heard of it."

"It's a port city on the Kotash Sea. They have a library that is second only to the Great Library in Might City and one of the only guilds of magic users in Ephriat." Conner stood then and stretched his arms high above his head, "We should be getting downstairs, the people of

Puko will want to send us off soon. We can finish this discussion after we leave."

Aleisha, Conner, and the five dragons gathered in the clearing awaiting the sendoff by the people of Puko. Aleisha sat atop Snarf's back and Conner spoke quietly to Ignatius, apparently attempting to smooth over the bad relations that had been stirring since their arrival. Locke, standing mere feet from his father, occasionally sent a hateful glare in Aleisha's direction, but never spoke a word loud enough for her to hear. After what seemed like hours to Aleisha, Ignatius and his son stepped away from Conner and turned to the trees, from whence hundreds of dark skinned people emerged.

The scene was so similar to the day they arrived, yet so different as the people of Puko did not send them off with the same warmth as they had greeted them. Aleisha wished that their stay could have been different, but she knew that as long as they expected her to take Gabriel's place as Briganti's babe, and as long as she refused to accommodate their wishes, she and her friends would never be welcome here.

"Let us send our," Locke glared one last time at Aleisha, "friends on their journey. We have a duty to aid them as best we can to prepare for their travel to an unknown land. Let us bring supplies and food to aid in their journey and let us pray for their safety as they depart. We are honored that our guests found our humble home a fitting resting place in these past days, and now we must see to it that they find it an equally pleasant place to leave." As he finished his speech, many of the citizens of the forest town approached Conner and handed sacks of various shapes and sizes to him, which he placed in much larger saddlebags that had been secured on the sides of the twin dragons. Once the final sack was placed on Grizwald's wing, Conner moved toward Ignatius. Giving the older man a friendly embrace, he nodded and spoke too quietly for Aleisha to hear before turning to Fortuna. Aleisha could see tears in her gentle eyes as she hugged Conner. With farewells said, Conner nodded respectfully to the crowd one last time and climbed onto his horse's back, directing it to leave the clearing and move into the dense forest away from the familiar trees of Puko.

As soon as Conner disappeared into the foliage, Byron raised his great wings into the air and lifted his large form into the sky. Each dragon followed suit, leaving Snarf and Aleisha to exit last. The last image of Puko Aleisha saw was Briganti pulling her cloak from his robe and holding it before him to remind her of the dangerous secret she could not hide from her companions forever.

As the trees shrank beneath her, Aleisha finally began to truly relax for the first time since learning of her origin.

Chapter 15

After flying a few miles out of the forest, the dragons landed in a large field of clover. Aleisha slid down from Snarf's back and began walking through the tall grass and weeds to look for anything she could use for fuel to start a small fire. She figured that they would be stopped for quite some time while waiting for Conner to catch up on his horse, and she planned to heat some of the stew that the villagers had sent with them for dinner. While searching through the thousands of purple clovers for anything resembling wood, she listened half-heartedly to the dragons behind her as they shared in their usual brotherly camaraderie.

Grizwald and Snarf, being the two least mature of the dragons, were constantly finding ways to annoy their brothers with silly pranks and stupid jokes while Grezald would laugh heartedly at anything they said or did and Dagmar would try to look frustrated by their infancy, all the while Byron would watch silently, like a wise parent watching over his sons. Aleisha had often noted the familial companionship of the dragons and how easily Conner joined them. She had often wondered how long Conner had been a part of the group, or if he had been raised with them instead of his natural family. She supposed that since he was a Dragonsoul he could have been placed with them by his Dictator, though she doubted that they would have allowed any human to interfere with their family uninvited.

Several hours passed and Aleisha had long since given up on finding any good fuel for her fire. The only thing

144

to be found in the field was grass and weeds, nothing would hold a flame long enough to heat the dinner she had hoped for, but she had a suspicion that, if she asked, Conner could teach her some way to heat the stew with her magic. She wasn't sure why she was so uncomfortable with the idea of using her power for such a menial task, but she suspected it had a lot to do with not wanting to become dependent on her power; she had lived her whole life not even knowing she had it and didn't want to swing to the opposite extreme of becoming consumed by it.

"It appears that our young Dragonsoul has finally decided to join us," Aleisha noticed that Snarf's voice was louder than it had been in the past hours, almost as if allowing her to hear him, made his voice that much clearer.

"Oh, shut up. You know that this horse doesn't move as fast as you do." Conner jumped down from his horse and traipsed over to Byron's side. "I can't understand why they always have to be so difficult. Is it really necessary for me to trudge through that accursed forest every time I leave their sorry little village?"

"They have always seen it as an insult to simply vanish from the forest. The only reason that we are allowed to fly out is because they don't want our large forms to destroy their precious foliage." Byron responded to his outburst with his usual calm voice.

"They just like to show off their beautiful home," Grizwald would not be satisfied if he didn't add a sarcastic comment to every conversation, and Aleisha was pleased to hear that his voice had the same added clarity as Snarf's voice when he allowed her to hear him.

She could use this new discovery to her advantage; all she had to do was make sure she only responded when she heard the clarity, and never react when she didn't, and they might never figure out about her Darksoul trait.

"I was attacked by that same stupid snake I told you about last time."

"That's hardly likely, as the last time was so long ago that any snake that attacked you then would be long dead by now."

"I'm telling you it was the same snake. It remembered me."

"How can you tell if a snake remembered you?" Snarf was trying to crack a joke, but Conner's expression said clearly that he wasn't amused.

"It knew how to avoid my attacks, like it had battled me before."

"Could it be a puppet of Tallen?" Dagmar was still trying to hide his thoughts from Aleisha, but she wasn't sure if she succeeded in hiding her response to her father's name.

"Why would he send a snake to guard my exit from the forest?" he shook his head at the idea, as if dismissing it, "That doesn't make any since."

"Well I hope you killed it this time, whatever the reason for its existence," with that final word from Byron, the discussion was closed.

"What do we have to eat? Aleisha must be starving."

"Me? What about you? You just endured an epic battle." She was pleased by the eruption of laughter from the twins and the soft chuckle from Snarf that her comment received. She had never been able to make anyone laugh before; that wasn't her job.

146

"I'm a Dragonsoul; I have less of a need for food than you do."

"Do you realize that that makes no sense? Dragons need to eat more than people do, so if you are more like dragons than most people are, you should need to eat more. And besides, for all you know, I'm a Dragonsoul too."

"I told you that was just you," Grezald turned his head toward Aleisha, *"He's always said that he doesn't eat much because he's a Dragonsoul, but I always believed that he was just unusual."*

"Back to my question," Conner sent his orange friend an annoyed look, "What do we have to eat?"

"There is an abundance of breads, fruits, and stews. I was planning on heating some of the stew, because I figured that it would go bad the fastest, but I couldn't find anything to start a fire."

Conner offered her one of the most ridiculous grins she had ever seen as all five dragons burst out into varying levels of laughter, "Do you realize that that makes no sense?" he quoted her earlier comment in a gently mocking voice, "Did you try asking one of the five fire-breathing dragons?"

"Don't even they need some sort of fuel to keep the fire going once it's started?" She was a little embarrassed that she had not thought of that; she had been wandering around like a fool and the answer to her dilemma had been literally sitting right in front of her for hours.

"No one said we have to have a traditional campfire to cook our food." Conner walked over to Grizwald and began digging through one of the enormous saddlebags until he found one of the clay containers filled with stew. After bringing the container over to Byron, he held it away from his body, as if placing it on an unseen shelf. Giving it a look of mild concentration, he stepped away, leaving it suspended in midair. When Conner was a safe distance away, Byron opened his mouth and let out a thin, concentrated stream of flame, heating the suspended container of stew in just a few moments better than a campfire would have in an hour. As soon as Byron closed his mouth, Conner stepped back up and grabbed the bowl without so much a wince when his hands connected with the hot container.

Conner appeared quite pleased with himself for thinking of such a clever way to heat the stew as he offered her the steaming bowl, "Careful, it's very hot."

Aleisha cautiously reached out to touch the clay bowl, only to jerk her hand back in pain as the heat scorched her fingers. *"Well, I suppose that rules out Dragonsoul, the heat wouldn't bother you,"* Snarf sounded disappointed as if he was admitting defeat. *"I suppose you must be a Lightsoul then."*

"Or a Darksoul," Dagmar sounded like he was trying to start another argument, but this time no one bothered to pay him any attention. Only Aleisha seemed bothered by the accusation. She wished that she could explain to them that he was right without endangering their trust in her, but she realized now what Briganti had meant about her troubles following her; she would eventually be found out and the only way to save her friends' trust in her would have been to tell them as soon as she had learned the truth. They would learn that she was a

148

Darksoul, and they would know that she had lied to them. She would lose the only friends she had ever had.

Conner set the bowl on a sack of bread that he had retrieved from the saddlebags in order to give it a makeshift table. "Don't let him bother you so much. He's always been extremely suspicious. It's his way of showing that he cares. He is our unofficial protector," Conner chuckled as he spoke fondly of his adopted brother. "The sun is beginning to set; we should eat so that we can get some rest before dawn."

Aleisha was pleased to discover how easy it was to fall back into the routine of the quiet nights she had so enjoyed before their arrival in Puko. She had sorely missed Snarf's soft, warm wings while sleeping in her bed.

Morning came as it always did, with Aleisha stretching her tired muscles in the fortress of Snarf's wing. Conner was already up. He seemed to already be awake no matter how early she rose. "Mornin' Aleisha." He offered his usual smile and whatever remnants of the food they had brought for breakfast. It had been two weeks since they had left Puko and Aleisha was certain that they were lost, but every time she asked about it, Conner would assure her that he knew exactly where they were.

"What are we eating today?" she didn't really care much about the food, but her stomach was growling as it always did when she woke, and she had thought that they had eaten the last of the supplies the night before.

"I found one last loaf of Garret's bread, and I also have a rabbit cooking if you're willing to be a little patient."

They had long since left the seemingly endless field of clover and Conner had been enjoying manning the campfires since they were now able to find a good supply of kindling to keep one going.

"I don't mind waiting. When do you think we will reach Fonishia?"

"We should arrive by sundown," he never took his eyes off the rabbit as he slowly turned it over the flames. "Do you see those trees?" he tipped his head slightly in the direction of a line of trees about a mile to the south, "Fonishia is on the other side of those woods."

"It's not another forest village like Puko, is it?" Aleisha was not fond of the idea of staying in another town where she would be expected to eat with hundreds of other people, sleep in a room that had only a curtain for a door, and in which she had no privacy or anonymity.

"No," Conner chuckled at her obvious distaste of their previous residence, "We'll be flying over the bulk of the woods, but a few stray trees will be scattered throughout the town."

"As soon as you two finish your breakfast, we can head out," Byron had been circling above them, presumably scoping out the path ahead, and was now landing as he spoke.

Almost immediately after Byron finished speaking, Conner pulled the rabbit meat from the spit and handed one of the large chunks of meat to Aleisha, claiming one for himself and passing the rest to Byron, who snatched it out of the air and swallowed it whole. Aleisha savored her breakfast for a few moments before folding the remaining meat and partial loaf of bread in a thick cloth and placing it in her sack to save it for lunch.

Seeing that she was finished eating, Conner mounted Byron's back and waited as Aleisha climbed up Snarf's neck, which he had lowered for her to use as a ramp onto his back. The moment she was settled in between the shoulders of her large friend, all five dragons lifted themselves into the sky and headed toward the trees. From so high up, Aleisha loved to watch the horizon for signs of their next destination, but even now, she could not glimpse Fonishia past the trees that dominated the horizon for miles.

For hours, Aleisha sat quietly on Snarf's back and listened to the sound that his wings made as he sped through the air. She enjoyed watching as Grizwald and Grezald chased each other through the clouds and raced the occasional flock of birds that they would come across on their journey. It was entertaining to watch them pretend to struggle to keep up with the much smaller creatures, only to dart ahead of them when they got tired of following. Snarf would occasionally move to join the twins but would always catch himself and return to follow diligently behind Byron and Dagmar as they continued at a steady pace over the huge forest.

Having finished the rest of her breakfast once her stomach began grumbling again, Aleisha lay back between Snarf's shoulders and closed her eyes to rest. If she could sleep for a few minutes while atop of the great beast, then maybe she would not be too tired to explore a little once they reached Fonishia.

Listening to the steady beating of wings and feeling the rush of wind every time his powerful wings forced the air down around her, Aleisha slid back in time to her first flight with the dragon. How different that ride had been; how terrified yet how excited she had been to be lifted from captivity in Cedrick's mansion. How long ago that felt. She could barely remember being the scared, powerless girl, trapped in a life of servitude to a man who saw her beauty as her only value, as a trophy to be shown off to his powerful friends. How different she was now that she was free. Now that she had discovered her power. Now that she feared something much more terrible than a cruel old drunk.

"Aleisha," she was vaguely aware of someone in the distance calling her name. "Aleisha," the voice called again, gently pulling her toward consciousness, "we're here." Finally opening her eyes, she saw that Conner was sitting in between Snarf's shoulder blades, her normal seat, looking down at her sleeping form stretched over his spine. "Welcome to Fonishia."

Chapter 16

As she raised her head, she saw a dozen small buildings made of stone scattered in a seemingly random pattern inside a high wall. Every house looked identical and they each had one door with a small porch and two seats on each porch. The fronts of the houses all pointed away from the wall around the tiny village. At the center was one large building with a huge stable that could have easily housed two or three dozen horses. Two small trees grew on either side of the center building and a short man was standing on the porch watching them. "This is Fonishia?" she had expected it to be a lot bigger; she didn't even see a building that could have been the library that Conner had mentioned.

"This is a very small section of Fonishia. This is an inn of sorts; a wealthy man from Might City built this as a place for travelers and seamen to stay in relative comfort and privacy as an alternative to the boarding houses you would find in most towns." He helped her down from Snarf's back and turned her toward the center building as the dragon lifted himself into the air and flew out of the inn; there was not enough room inside the wall for the dragons to rest comfortably, and the others had apparently already left in search of a more suitable place for them to stay. "Titus has agreed to give us a room while we remain in Fonishia."

Titus waited patiently on the porch of the large building, which turned out to be the dining hall for any guests of the inn and also served as a permanent residence for many of the workers that manned the inn.

"Welcome, welcome," the old man spread his arms in greeting as he addressed the two, "I am honored to have such brave warriors stay at my humble inn. Please come with me." As he turned to show them inside, Aleisha gave Conner a questioning look.

"He thinks that anybody who rides a dragon is a brave warrior," he leaned close to her so as not to be overheard as they stepped into a large room filled with rows of tables occupied by hungry seamen. "Don't bother trying to correct him; I've tried every time I come here." Titus led them through the crowded room into an office in the back of the building.

"I've already told my stable boy where to put your horse once it arrives," the old man smiled as he pulled several drawers open, clearly looking for something, "I can have him bring some food to your cabin if you would prefer not to eat with the men; they tend to get a bit rowdy and I don't think such a lady as yourself would appreciate their, um, energy." Having located what he was searching for, he handed Conner an iron key and led them back into the dining hall where a large, muscular man with no shirt immediately stepped between Titus and his guests.

"What's this, someone bring a tramp?" the man's breath reeked of the alcohol that was being served with his dinner, "I do hope you're planning to share. Nobody likes a hog." Much to Aleisha's horror, the entire room erupted into drunken cheers as Conner stepped protectively in front of her, blocking her from their view.

"Finley. Sit down," Aleisha could barely see the top of a man's head appear over Conner's shoulder. "Sit down and finish your supper. No one cares to listen to your unsavory voice." Finley turned and growled at the man but returned to his seat without argument. "You would be wise to avoid showing your face inside these walls, ma'am. The men here have no sense of decency." The stranger spoke loudly enough for those seated nearest to them to hear his insult.

"Yes, we noticed that." Conner spoke quietly and deliberately in response to the man in front of him.

"You needn't be suspicious of me Conner," at the sound of his name on a stranger's lips, Conner widened his stance, as if preparing to strike. "Elam sent me; he ordered me to bring you to him."

"You know Elam?" Aleisha stood on her toes, trying to see more of the strange man from behind Conner's large form; she was just able to make out the color of his red hair as he nodded to Conner's inquiry. "We should continue this elsewhere."

"I agree. My room is just outside the dining hall." Conner moved to follow the man, finally offering Aleisha a chance to see him. The well-dressed stranger was slightly shorter than her and thinner than any man she had met before. His long, fiery-red hair hung past his shoulders and boasted a healthy shine that would make most women jealous. He walked like a man of authority, and when he turned to open the door, she could see that he had a long and serious face, but he looked much too young to have the confidence and authority he had shown in his encounter with Finley. There was something oddly familiar about the young man, though Aleisha was sure she had no way of knowing him. Most likely, his haughty attitude simply reminded her of

Cedrick; whatever the case, she immediately disliked him.

The stranger's room was, in fact, right outside the dining hall; it was the first house to the right of the large building and only a short distance from the stable as well. As soon as the door to the tiny house was closed, Conner reclaimed his protective stance in front of Aleisha, "Who really sent you?"

"I told you, Elam sent me." He did not sound at all alarmed by Conner's accusatory tone.

"He didn't know we were coming."

"Conner," the stranger spoke as if addressing a child, "you know very well that the Librarian has ways of knowing these things without you telling him. He sent me to be sure that you and Aleisha arrive safely and made your way to him in a timely fashion; he knows how you like to dawdle sometimes."

Aleisha could see Conner's shoulders relax as he stepped away from her, grabbing her hand to lead her to a seat next to him.

"Thank you," The man exhaled heavily, as if he had just completed an arduous task, "now can we get to business?" at Conner's short nod, he pulled a wooden seat with thick arms from the desk near the back window and sat with his legs crossed, splaying his silk cape over the arms in an exaggerated show of grandeur. "My name is Syris, Elam's apprentice."

"What happened to Qim?" Conner interrupted Syris midsentence.

"He left Fonishia almost ten years ago to begin a family. You remember Anna of course; Qim wed her and they left the city soon after. I believe they settled somewhere in the Waves of Might." At his conclusion, Syris raised an eyebrow at Conner, as if seeking permission to continue his earlier thought.

"Elam said that you have found a young traveler," Syris looked directly at Aleisha as he spoke, "a girl with an unreadable map. The librarian is intrigued by your mother's map and has already begun research on possible spells and codes she may have had placed on it."

"When will we see him?" Conner drew the man's glare for a second time as he spoke.

"We will leave first thing in the morning; Elam is apparently very eager to meet with you again, Conner." Aleisha could not tell if she heard suspicion or jealousy in the apprentice's voice.

"Good, we'll be ready at dawn." With that, Conner stood and reached for Aleisha's hand again, pulling her out the door behind him as he hurried toward a cabin located near the wall of the inn.

As soon as they stepped onto the porch of the small cabin, he let go of her hand to place the key that Titus had given him into the lock on the door. The wooden barrier swung open without a noise to reveal a sparsely furnished residence identical to the one they had just left. The only furnishings in the room were a narrow couch that sat up against the front wall, a small table in the center of the room with a vase of dead flowers, a desk with one chair sitting at a large window at the back wall of the cabin, and a narrow bed sat up against the north wall. A small arched doorway on the south wall led to a cramped dining area that boasted a shallow counter stalked with a water pitcher and a few pewter cups. Conner stalked over to the counter and snatched up one of the cups, dumping some of the water from the pitcher into his mug before slurping the liquid and slamming it back onto the counter. "You don't seem thrilled by Syris' report."

"Elam shouldn't have known about the map; it's true that he sometimes seems to know things before it should be possible, but no one knew about that map other than you, me, and my brothers." Conner paused and lifted his hand to his neck, scratching it as he contemplated the situation, "Did you mention it to Briganti?"

"No, I never trusted him with anything." Aleisha watched him for a few more seconds as he paced in front of her, "Why does it matter that Elam knew about the map?"

"Because he shouldn't have had any way of knowing, the only way I can think of him finding out would be if your old master had made known that he was looking for you, but even then, I can't see why he would have let on that the map was enchanted." He shook his head as a heavy sigh escaped his lungs, "I don't trust what should not be, and he should not have known about your mother's map."

"Do you trust Elam, though?"

"Most of the time, he is not loyal to any one person or group of people, his friend today might be a stepping-stone tomorrow. All that truly holds his dedication is his quest for knowledge." He continued pacing most of the evening, muttering to himself as he did. Aleisha tried to go to bed early, but her long nap on the way prevented her from getting any sleep.

Chapter 17

Aleisha awoke to a dark room and the smell of cooking food. Rolling onto her side, she looked across the small room at the made bed that Conner had occupied the night before. He had insisted that she take the couch, claiming that it was both quieter and more comfortable; she had been made grateful for the suggestion as soon as he sat on the bed. The dreadful creaking sound it made with each movement would have kept them both awake all night from her constant turning, but he somehow managed to stay perfectly still, at least until she fell asleep. She couldn't even begin to guess how he had gotten out of the horrid thing, as well as straighten the sheets, without waking her.

Letting out a very unladylike groan, she rolled clumsily off of the couch and slumped over to the counter, ignoring Conner's pleasant greeting, and grabbed the pewter cup that she had seen him fill with water. "Ready at dawn," Aleisha mumbled as she slurped her water, "ready at dawn was a dumb thing to say." Through her morning grogginess, she heard him chuckle at her moments before a loud banging sounded on the door, causing her to drop her cup.

Conner strode toward the door and pulled it open to reveal Syris standing on the porch with an expectant expression, "You said you would be ready," he pushed past Conner and stepped into the small room, surveying his surroundings with distaste; as if his identical room was somehow better for the sole reason that it was his.

"I said we would be ready at dawn, the sun is not yet up," Conner glared at the intruder as he sniffed the air around him, as if judging the quality of their morning meal and finding it lacking.

"In any case, I am prepared to go. With or without you," raising one eyebrow in an arrogant display of superiority, Syris looked from Conner to Aleisha and back again, as if expecting them both to hurry to obey his will.

"We said we would be ready at dawn," Conner's voice came out as a growl as he repeated himself and tried to usher the intruder out of the cabin. "You need not wait for us; I happen to remember my way to the library." Syris' arrogant expression melted into one of shock as Conner addressed him in such a disrespectful manner. Lifting his nose and throwing his shoulders back in an attempt to regain his poise, Syris made a strange grunting sound and sprawled himself into the nearest chair with forced elegance.

Munching on the eggs that Conner had been fixing when she awoke, Aleisha watched the strange confrontation from the kitchen. She had often witnessed behavior similar to Syris' while living in Cedrick's mansion, but she had never seen anyone so boldly defy such a person. Catching her eye, Conner winked and offered a mildly amused expression as the haughty fellow conceded for a moment.

She tried to enjoy her breakfast in silence, but every second Syris was made to sit seemed to make him even more impatient and made Conner even more determined to make him wait. After only a few minutes, the tension between the two men became nearly impossible to endure. "I'm ready to leave," shoving the end of her breakfast into her mouth, Aleisha rushed over to the couch and lifted her sack, "Do you need to get your horse before we go?"

Conner stepped away from the door frame that he had been leaning on and took the bag from her hands, "Finally," Conner's usually kind expression darkened as they heard Syris speak. "I was beginning to think we would never begin our journey."

"Journey?" Conner leveled a bored expression at the man, "I would hardly call the distance from the inn to the library a journey."

"In any case, we should have left by now. Elam has been expecting us." With another great show of superiority, Syris marched out the door as Conner rolled his eyes and followed silently.

Riding on the back of Conner's horse, Aleisha leaned toward him, "What's Elam's story?"

"What do you mean?" Conner never moved his eyes from the back of Syris' head.

"How does he know we're coming? How does he know about the map? Why is he so mysterious and mystical?"

"Elam is the keeper of knowledge; he has taught some of the greatest minds in Elbot and is rumored to have read every book in the great library in Might City. He is also rumored to have magic, though no one has ever witnessed his use of it." Conner spoke as if reciting a memorized description of the old man. "He often knows things that he shouldn't, giving him the appearance of practicing divination."

"Do you think he'll help us?"

"We're here," Syris hopped down from his horse and gestured grandly at a stone building that towered over the surrounding structures, "The Library of Fonishia, one of the largest, most complete libraries in all of Elbot, rivaled only by the Great Library of Might City. All lovers of knowledge and seekers of wisdom find their way to her beautiful doors at some time in their lives."

"Syris," a booming voice, originating from a tall, slender man in a brown cloak interrupted Syris' speech, "These are not sight-seeing travelers in need of an introduction; they are pilgrims in search of the knowledge you so readily boast of. Bring them in." Elam spun around and stormed into his home, giving no opportunity to protest.

As impressive as Aleisha had found the library's exterior, it could not compare to the awe she experienced upon entering. The front room was furnished with several chairs dispersed in a random pattern all around the large room, each chair was accompanied by a small table with a lantern and at least one book sat on each table, many of the chairs also had books resting on the seats or the wide arms.

Passing through a wide archway, the ceiling disappeared as the room seemed to stretch infinitely upward. Every thirty feet, the wall boasted a narrow balcony to give readers access to the shelves. At each level, a sliding ladder was perched on the shelves to further aid in retrieving the desired volume. Spiral staircases led from one level to another and a large loading platform connected to a pulley system offered quicker access for those moving large loads of books at a time. In the center of the room was an enormous circular oak table with a large hole taken out of the center, where a rotating bench had been set up. Dozens of books were open and scattered on the table and a few stray pieces of parchment suggested that someone had been taking notes on whatever it was that they were reading.

Elam stepped onto the table with the aid of a stepstool set up near its edge and descended into the holed-out middle, claiming his seat on the rotating bench. He looked much older than any man Aleisha had ever met, though from her recent encounters with Conner and Briganti, she had learned not to try to guess age by appearance alone. His skin reminded her of drying leather; it was rough yet weathered, dark yet clear. He had a beard, like she had expected, but unlike Briganti's long white beard, he kept his trimmed short and well-groomed with areas of darker, almost black, hair. The old man gathered a few of his notes, as if preparing to go through them, "Why did you come, Conner?"

"I was under the impression that you already knew that." He boldly approached the circular table, an act which, by the look on Syris' face, was simply not done.

"Why don't you tell me anyway, for my amusement," the old man cringed as Conner picked up one of the pieces of loose parchment and began reading it.

"You have information on Aleisha's map, we need it."

"Map? I have heard of no map; why don't you tell me about it?" Aleisha glanced at Syris, expecting a reaction to his denial; he watched with a bored expression, as if he had witnessed similar exchanges several times before.

"You and I have played this game enough times before, Elam, but this time, I have no information to offer you except what your man Syris has revealed that you already know. So how about we skip the informational dump, and you simply help me find the solution to the girl's puzzle." Conner continued sifting through papers in front of him, even as the librarian glared at him. "Hmm, you don't seem to be having any more success than we have been having."

"No success?" The old man practically shouted as he threw himself out of his seat, "No success indeed, I have discovered a dozen possible answers to your query. I can't get any farther without seeing the map myself." Conner only nodded as he continued to read the loose papers in his hands.

"You seem to think it is encoded, you have at least four different coding books out here." Finally looking up from the notes, Conner nodded to Aleisha, bidding her to approach.

"Yes, I had heard that you were having trouble reading it, and that seemed the most likely reason. However, there is always the possibility that it was enchanted as well. Like I said, I will need to inspect the map myself in order to discern more."

Aleisha looked to Conner to seek permission to speak, on his answering nod, she turned to Elam, "My mother told me that the map is enchanted so that only I can read it. I don't think that it is coded, she would have had to teach me the code."

"Now this is new. Conner, why didn't you tell me it was enchanted?" He shrugged as the old man lunged over his work station and nearly ran for the loading platform, "I had gathered several materials on different spells of revelation and enchantments of concealment, but I was nearly convinced that such a map, left by a mere mortal for her mortal daughter, would not have been enchanted. Oh, the time I wasted when I rejected my initial guess. Ahh, here it is." The old man never stopped talking as he rummaged through the stacks of books on the platform, pulling several books out and placing them in separate stacks. "Now, Aleisha, is your mother the kind of woman who would have made this incredibly fancy and complex, or should I be looking for something so simple even the biggest of fools could figure it out while the most brilliant of minds will puzzle over it for days?"

"Um," she glanced desperately at Conner, she had no idea what her mother would have done to the map; she had been young when Cedrick bought her, too young to be able to intelligently predict how her mother would have handled the map.

"She didn't know her mother well enough to know that."

"Well then," Elam, with a large stack of books in his hands, walked back to the table and dumped the contents of his arms onto a relatively bare spot. "May I see the map?"

At Conner's short nod, Aleisha dug her mother's map out of her dress pocket. Walking up to the old librarian, she placed it carefully into his outstretched hand, "Thank you," he said softly, "I know it is hard for you to trust me since you don't know me yet, but try not to judge me by my apprentice," he winked then, "He's a weird one." She had to smile at the old man, maybe he wasn't as cold and unwelcoming as he had appeared. Turning back to the men in the room, he spoke back up, "Shall we have lunch? I missed breakfast doing research on a misplaced magic user."

Seemingly out of nowhere, a young boy came dashing into the room carrying a tray filled with an assorted variety of sandwiches. After they were all seated at one of the tables in the opening room, Elam passed out the sandwiches and some drinks, "Shall we thank the Maker before we eat?" each of them in turn bowed their heads and paused a moment in silence before Elam lifted his head to signal the end of the prayer. "I will study the map after we dine, perhaps by the morning I will have some answers."

"You mentioned a misplaced magic user," Aleisha ventured to ask, "What did you mean by misplaced?"

"It is nearly impossible to keep track of all magic users," he seemed simply elated that she had asked and delved into explanation without hesitation, "but I can usually track down any that have soul power if need be. Recently, the guild here came to need the expertise of one knowledgeable in a specific kind of magic, so I was going through possible candidates, you have to be very careful when seeking out the help of a Darksoul, dangerous bunch they are. Anyway, I realized a disturbing trend."

"You were seeking out a Darksoul to teach in the guild?" Conner slammed his cup onto the table.

"As I said, they needed certain expertise, and I was being very careful in my pick." Elam raised his eyebrows at Conner, showing clearly that he did not share Conner's concern and that he would not indulge

166

him in an argument, "Anyway, I noticed a trend that started about fifty years ago; Darksouls have been disappearing without explanation. There are at least half a dozen that have gone missing, and I simply cannot find them."

"But aren't Darksouls bad? So, their disappearance is a good thing, isn't it?" Aleisha looked from Elam to Conner, who suddenly looked as worried as Elam, only Syris seemed unconcerned by the dwindling Darksouls.

"Yes, Darksouls are known to be the most dangerous magic users of all, but I'm not suggesting that specific Darksouls are disappearing and not being found. These Darksouls are dying just like everybody else; they have funerals, their Dictators mourn for them, and a few even have families left behind. That is not what concerns me, what is truly bothersome is that I cannot find their replacements."

Aleisha still wasn't understanding the problem, "A Dictator will not simply neglect to choose a new babe, Aleisha," Conner stole her attention from the old man, "There should only be one reason for a Dictator to stop choosing a new babe," he looked hopefully at Elam.

"That was my first thought, the reason my list has only reached six missing Darksouls is that I have only verified six Dictators who seem not to have a chosen babe."

"So, Dictators are choosing Darksouls and then losing them? Or hiding them?" Aleisha did not like where this was going, Conner had no idea how close he was to the truth with that last statement. At least she hoped he had no idea.

"That's what I'm afraid of, I can't imagine why they would be hiding their babes. I'm afraid they may be preparing for another war." He shook his head sadly, and everyone ate in silence for several minutes.

"Wait," everyone at the table jumped when Conner spoke, "Are any others missing? Any Dragonsouls or Lightsouls?"

"Well, I don't know, I guess I hadn't thought of that. I will add that to my research list," with a final nod, Elam returned once again to his meal.

Chapter 18

After lunch was over, Syris led them to the back of the library, past the enormous room full of books, and into an elegant hallway lined with several spacious study rooms. "I think you will find this more comfortable than that horrid inn," Syris gestured to a pair of rooms that had been equipped with small beds next to the oversized reading desks. "I cannot even begin to guess how long Elam will be working on your map, so I suggest you make yourselves at home. You can either find yourselves something to read, or something else to keep yourselves busy because I am not here to entertain you." With that, he turned to leave them.

"Pleasant fellow," Conner huffed and strode over to the desk in the smaller of the two rooms. "I guess we should get our things, Elam is rarely as quick to find answers as he boasts; he is a very intelligent man, but sometimes his vast supply of knowledge can make it difficult to sift through all the garbage to reach the information he is looking for."

"Do you really think that the missing Darksouls are being kept hidden for a coming war?" He looked up in surprise when she spoke.

"Not necessarily, I'm not even ready to believe that all of these instances are related, but it is a curious phenomenon." Walking back to the entrance, he ushered her farther into the room and closed the door, "I'm not going to worry too much about the missing Darksouls. What really interests me is the prospect of finding your Dictator."

"Not me," Aleisha desperately searched for an excuse to get him away from this dangerous path, "You don't trust or even seem to like your Dictator, why would mine be any better?"

"You would benefit greatly from being trained by your Dictator, they would be better than me at training, and not as aggravating as Briganti."

"But," she lowered her head, searching her thoughts for a possible way out, "what if Elam can't find any Lightsoul Dictators missing their babes?" Suddenly terrified she had slipped up, she jerked her head up to see his compassionate expression.

"That's what you're worried about?" he barely whispered his response, "You aren't a Darksoul, Leish. You have too much good in you."

"You don't know that, what about my anger problems?" she couldn't imagine why she was suddenly trying to convince him; she didn't want him thinking she was a Darksoul.

"No one is perfect. Just because you've gotten angry a few times, doesn't mean you're evil. It means you're human." He gently gripped her shoulder and led her out of the room, "Everyone camped right outside the city last night, why don't we go check on them?"

Aleisha followed Conner through the streets of Fonishia; he seemed to know exactly where he was, and often pointed out the major landmarks so that she would not be totally lost, were they to get separated. "Is there anywhere you haven't been?" At Conner's strange expression, she elaborated, "You have mentioned you were in Shiloh when you had the vision about me; you had obviously been to Puko on several occasions before we went there, you know Fonishia quite well, and from a few comments you've made, I would guess you have been to Might City. You just seem to travel a lot and I wondered if you've made it to every town in Ephriat."

"No, I've been to several of the large cities and countless small villages, but I have avoided a few places that I hope never to find myself."

"Such as?"

"The Mountains of Ban and everything beyond them. Only Ban worshipers travel to that part of the continent. Only Ban worshipers and their next sacrifices." His tone indicated a deep disgust for the followers of the false god, but she also thought she heard something close to pity in his voice.

"If you are trying to exit the city along a road, make sure you take a gate that has this symbol on it," he pointed to a small sign depicting a horse and rider, "If it doesn't have this, it leads to the port." Passing through the gate, Aleisha saw a large orange shape moving to her right. As Grezald landed, Conner and Aleisha turned off of the road to meet the great beast.

"I have been sent to escort you to the others," He bowed his long neck in a show of mock elegance, then chuckled and stretched to let them climb on. *"Grizwald wanted to come, but I insisted because I am the better flyer."*

Both humans chuckled as he lifted them into the air, *"So, does Elam have any bright ideas about Aleisha's map?"*

"He's working on it as we speak, but I'm not sure how much help he'll be this time; he asked Aleisha for some information about her mother to narrow down his search, so it sounds like he's already got too many viable solutions to be helpful."

"Did he have an opinion about Aleisha's soul power?"

"We didn't ask. He doesn't know she has magic, and I'd like to keep it that way." Grezald lowered himself to the ground when they neared the other four dragons. As soon as their feet touched the grass, every voice was raised in welcome. After everyone had calmed down a bit and Conner and Aleisha were allowed to get comfortable, Conner described in detail how their stay in Fonishia was going thus far.

"So, you think we can find a list of possible Dictators that could be Aleisha's." Byron studied her with an almost parental stare, *"Do you want to seek your Dictator out, Aleisha? We will assist in any way we can if you do."*

Aleisha looked around the group of dragons, then at Conner, who offered her an encouraging nod. "If my Dictator wanted anything to do with me, he should have revealed himself," she felt awful lying to her friends, but they had her backed into a corner with this offer, "and I can't imagine that any Dictator could be a better teacher, friend, or mentor than I have found in this group." At least that part was true, she had come to really trust this small group of friends; she only wished that she could trust them with her only secret.

"It is decided then, we will not pursue your Dictator," Dagmar seemed to surprise everyone in the group with his quick agreement; Aleisha had certainly expected his usual protests and accusations, *"You are a part of our*

family now; if we will not force Conner to face his Dictator, we cannot force you to seek yours."

"Hear that?" Snarf nudged her gently with his nose, *"Even Dagmar has accepted you."* The blue dragon nodded in affirmation, sending Aleisha's conscience into a nosedive. She had finally managed to get Dagmar on her side, and she had never felt so wretched in her life.

Chapter 19

"Hey Leish, get up. Elam thinks he's found something." Aleisha groaned as she tried to drag herself out of bed. Conner pounded on the door again, "Come on, he's waiting." She managed to roll out of bed and landed on the floor with a clumsy thump; Conner laughed from the other side of the door. Pulling herself up with the aid of the bedpost, she managed to tear her dirty clothes off and replace them with her last remaining clean dress; pulling her brush through her hair, she tried to ignore Conner's continued calls for speed. "Come on, Alei-," she pulled open her door, stopping him mid-word, "Mornin' Leish," he grinned.

"You are too awake for this early in the morning," he chuckled again, taking great pleasure in watching her stagger past him like a drunk. "And since when do you call me 'Leish'?"

He shrugged, grinning at her as he grabbed her arm to stabilize her as she walked, half-asleep, down the hallway, "It just seems to fit, more casual. You know? Signifies our change from formal acquaintances to trusted friends." He handed her a muffin and continued to speak as she shoved it into her mouth, "Elam stayed up all night reading about possible enchantments your mother could have had the map enchanted with. He sent Syris to wake me up over an hour ago, so you should be happy I let you sleep so long. Anyway, he made an extensive list of enchantments that she could have used, but I think he's leaning toward a keyspell."

"What's that?" Aleisha blushed and covered her mouth as she nearly spit her muffin at him as she spoke.

"A keyspell is just what it sounds like; whatever that particular kind of spell is used on can only be accessed by a particular person, use a specific 'key' as chosen by the magic user that cast the spell." Entering the main library, Aleisha saw Elam sitting on his bench, pouring over a large manuscript.

"Aleisha." The old man sprang out of his seat and nearly leapt over his table, "I think I've found the answer."

"Conner told me about the keyspell." Elam glared at Conner, "How do we figure out what the key is?"

The old man seemed to deflate a bit at hearing that he wouldn't get to explain. "That is the problem," he shrugged, "There is no way to discover the key except to experiment. This is the thing that worries me; many of the most common keys would destroy the map if we try the wrong one." Aleisha gave him a questioning look, encouraging him to continue, "One of the favorite keys is to have the keyholder wash the item with a specific recipe. Unfortunately, we have no idea what the recipe would be, and you cannot simply wash your map over and over. In fact, if you wash this map at all, unless that is the key, it will probably ruin it anyway; the ink is not of high enough quality that it would withstand the water."

"So, we're no closer now than we were when we began." She knew it shouldn't matter so much to her now. After all, as a Darksoul, she was looking at her life in terms of centuries rather than decades, and she wasn't sure she should be pursuing eternal life anyway, since she was so full of the potential for evil. But Conner deserved the Elixir, he was good and had his brothers to live for, dragons who would look at his six or seven hundred years and see just a season of their lives. They deserved for Conner to have the Elixir.

"There is one way to find the key," Elam sounded like he was apologizing; she must have been showing her disappointment, "We could ask your mother."

Of course! Her mother chose the key, of course she would know what the key would be. Aleisha could feel herself lighten as an excited grin spread across her face. She hadn't even thought of it before, but she now had the power to save her mother from her cell. She was sure Conner and the dragons would help her, and Tallen was rarely at the castle, so she wouldn't have to worry about running into him.

Conner chuckled at her excitement, "Where would we find her?" She could feel her entire body almost wilt in response to his question.

"I don't know," she closed her eyes, trying to remember her ride from the castle to Cedrick's mansion. It had been too long ago, she had been too young, there was no conceivable way she would be able to remember. "I don't know. She would still be at the castle that we were held in, but I can't even begin to tell you where that would be."

"Hey, Leish," she felt Conner's hand on her shoulder again as he whispered reassuringly to her, "It's ok, we're not done trying. We'll figure something out." Elam handed her mother's map to her, "I can send Dagmar, Grezald, and Grizwald to scope out the land for this castle if you can give them any kind of description. Or, you could even," he stopped suddenly, turning his head as if he was watching some unseen creature.

"Conner," she grabbed his arm, pulling him back into the present, "I could even what?" He grinned and reached for her hand, pulling her behind him as he hurried out of the room, leaving Elam and Syris to stare after them in confusion.

On leaving the library, he led her to the stable, reaching immediately for his horse. "We will find your mother, Aleisha, this isn't about the Elixir anymore," he mounted the horse and quickly pulled her up behind him, "I saw your face when Elam mentioned finding your mother; she is more important than some silly potion."

As they sped through the city and toward the gate, Aleisha could not believe what she was hearing. She would never have thought that someone could be as selfless as Conner; he didn't even care about his own gain when he saw another's need. She had seen it in how quickly he had agreed to rescue her from Cedrick, his protection of her from his own when Dagmar had accused her, even his insistence on staying another night in a village that had not been kind to them only to keep from offending them.

When they neared the gate, a young boy opened it for them so that Conner would not have to stop. Galloping through the opening, Conner took them outside of Fonishia and rode along the tree line until Dagmar suddenly appeared out of nowhere next to them. She had never noticed how well his blue and white coloring helped him blend into the sky as he flew. "We need to get to the clover field."

"Of course," Snarf landed next to Dagmar and nodded a greeting to Aleisha and Conner, *"I'll take Aleisha, Snarf will carry you."* Snarf, Conner, and Aleisha all looked at Dagmar in surprise. *"We need to get to know each other a little better and I haven't been as welcoming as I should have been."* Conner nodded and turned to Aleisha, winking at her before he strode over to Snarf and climbed on his back.

Aleisha climbed onto Dagmar's back, settling in between his shoulder blades to get comfortable. "So," she began cautiously, "what did you want to talk to me about?"

They flew in silence for a few minutes, causing Aleisha to grow slightly apprehensive. *"I've been hard on you, and I want you to understand why."*

"Conner mentioned you are protective of your family."

"Yes, I am protective, and I know that some of my brothers are quick to accept and slow to reject. In my mind, you posed a threat, especially to Snarf and Conner; Snarf has always been too trusting, and I knew Conner would grow to enjoy having another human around," they reached the clover field, but Dagmar did not land, circling the small group of dragons below, he continued, *"When we learned that you had magic, I knew that Conner would want to train you; he thinks that anyone with power should know how to use it, thinks it goes toward safety and responsibility. I didn't think it was safe or responsible to train you if you turned out to be a Darksoul, but it has become clear that you are not consumed by evil, as most Darksouls are. And, whether it was intentional or not, you have ingrained*

yourself so deeply into our family that there will be no getting rid of you.

"So, as far as I'm concerned, it no longer matters what you are; you are family and I will protect you as I do my brothers." Having said his piece, Dagmar began his descent.

"Thank you, Dagmar," she couldn't think of anything else to say. She had finally succeeded in winning him over. The sad irony was that he had distrusted her when she was hiding nothing, but now that she was lying to them all, he finally accepted her without reservation.

Chapter 20

"Aleisha needs to find her mother," Conner addressed the group as he paced, hands held firmly behind his back, "not only is she the only person who will be able to help her access the map, but she is a prisoner of the man who sold Aleisha into slavery. I think we should help find her and free her from her keeper's cruelty." Every head nodded and several of the dragons voiced their support of the venture, "The only problem is, she doesn't know where her mother is being kept." He explained his idea to have a few of the them fly around to look for the castle, "Or, if Aleisha is willing to, she could conjure up a replica of the castle using the clover in this field. That would at least give us the general shape of it, and, if she is able, maybe a few clues to its location."

"Do you think you can build your father's castle for us?" Byron addressed Aleisha directly, turning everyone's attention to her.

"I think so, I mean, I've done it before. In the desert, when I was daydreaming." She looked about nervously, she had only ever intentionally formed something once, when Conner had taught her how to connect with the water in Puko. Truthfully, she was a bit worried she wouldn't be able to form such a complex building with any great detail.

"Just focus on your most vivid memory from the castle and reach out to the field to become the grass. Just like you did with the water," Conner's reassuring words renewed her confidence and she nodded, indicating that

180

she was ready. Walking away from the group, she searched for her only memory of seeing the outside of the castle.

Cedrick had a strong grip on her arms and was carrying her out of the only home she had ever known and into an alien world. As he threw her mercilessly into the cart attached to his elegant carriage, she turned to catch one final glimpse of the great fortress that held her mother, her precious mother that she might never see again.

"There just isn't enough here," Byron broke into her thoughts, startling her into open her eyes. Before her was a picture of a little girl laying in a cart, looking at a set of steps. She pulled all around her, looking for any more clover, grass, or twigs to add to the sculpture.

"There isn't enough here," she echoed the thought that she wasn't supposed to hear, letting them all know that she couldn't offer them the description they needed. The structure collapsed, leaving a large pile where the steps of the keep had been standing a moment before. Aleisha lowered herself to the ground in defeat; she had allowed herself to hope for a few minutes that they could find her mother, and for that hope, she received failure.

"Hey, Leish," Conner sat next to her as she stared at the pile of debris, "you were doing great, just ran out of material, that's all." Aleisha pulled her knees to her chest and rested her head in her arms; she wouldn't listen to him trying to make light of her failure. There was no way she could form something that big unless they ventured all the way back to the Desert of Tyree, where she would have enough sand to form an entire village. "I was thinking that you would have plenty of material here, but we could always try something else."

"Yeah, you seemed to like working with water," As soon as Snarf spoke, Conner leapt up from the ground.

"That's right, we could go out into the Kotash Sea and let her form it with the water."

"An interesting proposal," Byron let out a low hum as he thought through the possibility. *"She would certainly have enough to work with, but don't you think that that would be a disturbance to the people of Fonishia?"*

"They are accustomed to crazy magicians messing with their daily lives. They probably won't even look twice at what they'll most likely see as some young guild magicians playing an annoying prank." Conner beamed at her as he finished; he seemed confident that he had found the perfect solution. "What do you say? You up for trying again?"

She almost laughed at his enthusiasm, and even found herself wanting to retry just to prove him right, just to make him proud of her. "Yeah, I think I should." Snarf let out an excited noise that sounded remarkably like a bark as he lowered his head for her to climb onto. In a matter of seconds, Conner had mounted Byron and all five dragons had lifted themselves into the air and were speeding toward the sea.

Aleisha was amazed by how different Fonishia looked from above. The towering library sat in the center of the city, with six major streets pointing out from the library, and dozens of minor streets branching off from them. She chuckled as she recognized the similarity the design had to a spider web. She also marveled at how peaceful the entire city looked from above. Walking the streets,

182

she had been witness to the business and rushed tone of the people in even the side streets.

Just outside the circular shaped city sat a smaller circular wall, which she recognized as the inn that they had stayed in their first night after reaching Fonishia. Just inside the water, nearly a dozen trade and travel ships waited in the dock as the crews prepared for departure. "Why aren't there any ships in use?"

"The big ships leave in early morning, and the fishermen work at night. The only people on the water right now are families enjoying the day and fellowshipping together." Snarf nodded to a small cluster of three boats, *"They look to be the only ones you need to be wary of."*

Byron and Conner dove toward the water, submerging for a few seconds before reappearing and settling on the surface much like any water fowl would. Conner let out an enthusiastic hoot as a blanket of water fell from all around him. Snarf danced above the water in anticipation as the other three dragons followed the example of their leader. "Please don't," the eager young dragon complied by slowly descending and settling calmly on the water.

Aleisha stood on Snarf's back, signaling for him to spread his wings to bridge the gap between him and Byron. "Leish," she looked up from the clear water as Conner spoke from the dragon's back, "use your most vivid memory, not the one you were using earlier. You were obviously struggling to remember the details."

"That was the only time I saw the outside."

"It doesn't matter," he smiled encouragingly at her, "remember the most familiar part of the castle. Connect with that memory like you connect with the water, let your subconscious build the surrounding parts of the structure based on the subtle clues you never even realized you were picking up on; rumors you heard whispered by the guards, glimpses of the dungeon outside your cell, then you might be able to incorporate other memories."

"I think I get it. Start small, then build on that." When Conner grinned and nodded, she turned to the water, pausing before choosing a memory to begin with. If she could hold the water close enough together, then she could step into the castle, hopefully making the construction easier. Concentrating on the wetness beneath her mount, she closed her eyes and breathed deeply.

She felt a surge of energy the moment she connected with the water, she had never tried to control so much at one time, this would be exhilarating and difficult. Opening her eyes, she stepped off of Snarf's wing and onto the solid surface of the water.

The walls of the cell she was born in were made of large stones. The outside wall had one small window with iron bars to keep even the smallest of prisoners from escaping. In one corner of the cramped cell, a wooden slab hung from the wall by two thick chains, forming the uncomfortable bed that she had shared with her mother. In the opposite corner sat a small pot for them to relieve themselves. Her mother paced slowly in front of the bars that served as the fourth wall.

"Aleisha, that's amazing, now let your subconscious take over where your memory ends." At Conner's gentle encouragement, Aleisha strode past her mother and pushed the cell door open, walking into the hallway, she looked around her, watching each cell form as she remembered her first walk through the dungeon. She quickly found the stairs that led out of the dungeon, and took that path through the guards' quarters, past the cellars, and through the heavy door that would lead her to the great hall where she had met her father. After stepping only far enough into the spacious room to be sure she had built the entire structure, she turned toward the front door and headed toward the courtyard.

She looked up at the ceiling, where a bird was lazily flying in circles toward the top, giving her a guide in estimating the height of the room. On either side of the grand entrance, she saw the impressive draperies that she had remembered from the great hall, what she had not realized, was that each wall had a wide set of stairs leading to the next level of the castle. Curious to see the next floor, she took the stairs to the right, suddenly remembering the guards discussing several guests who had at one point occupied the several bedchambers on this floor. At the top of the stares, six bedchambers sat on one side of a long hallway, on the other side appeared to be a large chapel. Passing by each of the unoccupied rooms, she reached for the door at the end of the hall. A narrow stairway greeted her, the tightly spiraling staircase ascending the side of the east tower.

After roaming her childhood home for a few more minutes, she made her way back to the great hall, figuring that it was the only area large enough for all five of the dragons to fit comfortably. She couldn't wait to see their reaction to her accomplishment. Even she was amazed by the details that she had remembered from rumors and stories she had heard from her cell.

As she stepped into the great hall, she noted that it seemed quite a bit darker than the last time she had been in the room, even though the huge chandelier was still lit with dozens of candles. Shrugging, she stepped further into the room only to stop when she saw Conner's expression.

Conner stared at her with an expression that was equally disbelief, pain, and anger. Unsure of what may have upset him, she turned to look behind her, thinking that maybe he was glaring at something she had missed. All she saw out of the ordinary was a trail of thick smoke. Thick, dark smoke that seemed to form a trail up the staircase she had just descended. *"When you transform into your true form, as all magic users do when using great amounts of power, you will be seen as wearing a cloak identical to the one in my hand,"* Briganti's voice echoed in her memory.

"No!" her hands flew to her plain brown dress and sunk into the material. She was suddenly wearing a gray-black gown that seemed to swirl around her as if made of smoke instead of fabric. The hem consisted of such thick smoke, that it spread around her, leaving a cloud behind her and dimming the light in the room where she stood. Stripped of her deceitful beauty to reveal the dark, horrible truth of her identity, she stood before her comrades in disgrace.

She raised her head slowly, hoping to see some chance for forgiveness in Conner's angry scowl. She saw none. "I," he shook his head once, silencing her. They both knew that in order for her to transform, she would have to have known that she was a Darksoul. They all knew now that she had been hiding from them. Had been lying to them. His torn expression said everything she never wanted to hear from him. All the pain she never wanted to cause him. All the hate she never wanted to receive from him. As his eyes, his kind, gentle, wise eyes, filled with anger and tears, he turned away from her and climbed onto Byron's back, never saying a word as they lifted into the air.

"Why?" Snarf's agonized plea tore into her conscience.

"Snarf, I,"

"Don't," the young dragon looked away from her, just barely failing to hide his first tears as they slid down his soft fur. A moment later, he too, lifted into the air and broke through the wall of water to escape her presence. The twins followed without a word, leaving only Dagmar behind to witness her collapse onto the floor as her first sob choked the air from her lungs.

After a few moments, even Dagmar beat his great wings and ascended into the air, breaking through the water a second before the entire structure caved in.

She sat on the floor of her father's great hall with her head in her hands, trying to block out the reality of what was occurring around her. Her greatest success, the impressive building of this castle, mocked her as her worst mistake. The only people she had ever called friends were now gone. As soon as she felt the fifth break in her beautiful masterpiece, as soon as she knew Dagmar would not be caught in the thousands of gallons of falling water, she let the structure collapse. She would let this castle, this prison that had already stolen everything from her, take the only thing she had left.

Because of her placement in the great hall, most of the water fell around her, splashing and soaking her, but never covering her in mighty waves of justice. Only the ceiling of the great hall rained on her before she let the floor beneath her return to the soft water of the Kotash Sea.

As soon as she felt the water close around her, she was ripped from the sea by huge talons. Blinking the water from her eyes, she looked above her to see a huge blue form. *"You are not allowed to give up that easily, Darksoul."* Dagmar spoke with his usual gruff manner, but this time she heard what sounded like compassion woven into his usual anger and frustration. *"You still have a mother to save."*

"Dagmar," she barely forced the name from her lungs before choking on another sob.

"You'll have to save her yourself after that little display. Conner and Byron especially would refuse to help you now, even if you were foolish enough to ask."

"You knew." She didn't ask. She didn't have to; he was the only one who hadn't looked surprised.

"Of course I knew, and they're all going to be feeling pretty foolish when they remember my constant protests." The great dragon swooped toward the dock, only slowing enough to place her, unharmed, on solid ground before darting back up toward the clouds.

"Do you think they will ever forgive me?" she shouted her thoughts as loudly as she could, hoping that he wasn't too far to hear her yet.

"I don't know, Aleisha. I just don't know." With that final word, he sped away from her.

She stood on the dock, breathing heavily with tears flowing freely down her cheeks, hardly noticing the sailors passing her and giving her strange looks. One man, a vaguely familiar man, walked up to her and said something. She ignored him. She felt like her lungs were being crushed by the force of her sobs, and she only wanted to find somewhere to hide. "Hey woman, I'm talking to you."

Finley, the rude man from the inn, stood before her, sober, but no less distasteful than the last time she had seen him. He made another rude comment that she wasn't listening to and grabbed for her arm that was again covered in the brown cloth that she had donned that morning. She shifted her eyes to look into his, sending him stumbling back several paces. The huge man looked terrified as he tripped over his own feet and landed on a crate. Gasping for air, Finley reached for his throat. She didn't want to release him.

"Aleisha," another vaguely familiar man, this one too old to be a sailor, suddenly stood next to her. "Aleisha, let him go." His voice sounded like Dagmar's; sympathetic but stern. "You don't want to validate your friends' fears concerning you."

With a final pained gasp, Finley stood and fled. Aleisha screamed. She had never felt anything so justly painful before. She could feel her throat scratching excruciatingly as her agony forced too much air out of her lungs. Every part of her being ached with the knowledge that she had just lost the only people in the world that had cared for her. Every part of her ached with the knowledge that it was her own fault. Everyone on the dock stopped and stared at the young girl as she let out an agonized wail from the deepest part of her, before collapsing into Elam's embrace.

Chapter 21

Aleisha didn't know how she had gotten back to the library, but she lay in her bed, sometimes sobbing uncontrollably, sometimes feeling nothing as she stared at the ceiling. How could she have been so careless? She should have realized how much power she would need to conjure up such a large and elaborate structure. She should have told them that she couldn't do it. She should have protected herself from their discovery of her secret. She had lost the only people who she had ever called friends. She had lost the only people who had ever loved her.

Did they really love her though? Would they have left her if they had loved her? No, she would not turn this on them. She was the only one to blame. She had lied to them by keeping her identity a secret and she had caused them unfathomable pain when she finally revealed herself. The simple fact that they left her instead of torching her on the spot, as they had once vowed to do to the next Darksoul they encountered, was proof that they had loved her. And she had betrayed them.

A soft knock sounded on her door just before Elam let himself in. "I'm sure you've figured out that I saw the castle, and I know you are one of the Darksouls I've been looking for." When she didn't respond, he stepped further into the room and sat next to her on the bed. "If you had told me that you were looking for Tallen's Castle, I could have given you a map, could have saved you the trouble."

Aleisha groaned and rolled over, hiding her face from the old man as she let out another agonized sob. "I'm sorry, Aleisha. I'm afraid I've never been good at offering comfort." He shifted and placed a hand on her shoulder, "I'll let you remain for a few days to mourn the loss of your friends, but then I must insist that you begin preparations for the next leg of your journey. I simply cannot allow you to give up before you reunite with your mother." When she did not acknowledge his words, he sighed and stood, leaving her room and quietly closing the door behind him.

Three days passed before she left her room to find something to eat. "Ah, so the Darksoul has finally decided to join us." Syris' cruel grin looked more like a snarl.

"Calm down Syris, she has had a rough couple of days," Elam glared at his rude apprentice before turning back toward Aleisha. "Welcome, we made plenty if you would like to pull up a chair."

"I'd rather eat in my room if that's ok." She really didn't want to socialize. She wasn't sure if she would ever be ready to again, not after how disastrous her last attempt had been.

"No, I'm afraid that won't do. Either you eat with us, or not at all." Elam waited for a moment, then shrugged and continued his dinner.

She almost turned around and headed back to her room, but her stomach constricted painfully, reminding her that she had not eaten in three days. She breathed deeply, letting out an exaggerated sigh before sitting down to join the meal.

"You'll need to learn how to fight," Elam's sudden statement caught her by surprise.

"What? Why?"

192

Dragonsoul

"Well, if you are going to have any amount of success on this rescue mission, you will probably end up fighting Tallen, or at least a guard or two. It's simply unrealistic to expect you can simply walk into his castle and take your mother back." The old man spoke as if stating the obvious to a senseless child.

"Tallen is rarely at the castle, and the guard he keeps is minimal to nonexistent." She reached for a second sandwich as she swallowed the last bite of her first.

"The last time you were there was more than twenty years ago, Aleisha. You have no way of knowing if the situation remains the same today. And in any manner, minimal guard is still guard and will still need to be disposed of." He sipped his drink as he studied her reaction, "You will begin training after dinner," with that, he stood and exited.

As soon as she was finished eating, Syris took her plate and nodded toward the back of the library. "He'll be waiting in the yard; I'll be joining you in a moment." She nodded and headed to the back door.

Outside, she found the librarian standing in the yard with a sword in each hand. "Come," he held the swords out to her, "choose your weapon." In his left hand, he held a shining xiphos, in his right, an old two-handed great sword. She took the great sword.

"I have fought before." The old man raised one eyebrow, "As a child. We used to reenact legendary battles when Cedrick wasn't watching; I'm actually quite good," she swung the huge weapon experimentally, frowning when she realized how heavy it was, "that is, I was quite good with the sticks."

He chuckled, "You will battle Syris when he appears." The old man found a bench nearby and sat just as Syris stepped outside, holding a cutlass in each hand.

"Have you ever battled an opponent with two swords before?" He did not give her a chance to answer before running at her, swinging wildly.

Aleisha lifted the great sword to block the first swing, stumbling back a step at the solid collision, causing the second swing to miss her completely. He didn't give her even a second to regain her footing before bringing one of his blades down in an arc toward her head. She blocked again, losing more ground as he advanced. With each sequential attack, Aleisha somehow succeeded in blocking, but continued to lose ground until Syris had her backed up against the library's rear gate. In desperation, she swung at her still-advancing opponent, causing him to back up a foot. Leveling a glare at him, she launched him back several feet, giving her a few moments to collect herself.

Breathing deeply, she lifted the sword in front of her and closed her eyes. Focusing on the cold metal of the sharp blade and the rough feel of the leather that was tightly wound around the hilt, she exhaled, letting her breath collide with the flat side of the blade. As soon as she could feel her breath tickling the sharpened edges of her weapon, she opened her eyes.

All at once, she remembered every battle this weapon had been a part of, as if she had been the one wielding it. Suddenly, this sword that had moments ago felt awkward and cumbersome in her hands, rested comfortably in her palms, perfectly balanced and beautifully crafted just for her.

194

In the moment she had taken to connect with her weapon, Syris had recovered himself. He now stood ten feet away from her, fury darkening his eyes. When she chose to use magic on him, she shifted this fight from training to battle. The angry apprentice spun his cutlasses around his wrists, resetting himself for combat. Spinning as he approached her, he swung the blades around his body, bringing them towards her from both sides. She blocked both blades. She wasn't sure how she had managed it, but one of his cutlasses was sent flying out of his hand while she slammed the other into the ground. Pulling the hilt up, she hit him in the head with enough force to send him stumbling back once more, this time causing him to pause before his next attack.

Syris stood for a moment, glaring at Aleisha before lunging toward his fallen sword. She took advantage of the opportunity to attack and swung her sword down towards him as he picked up his weapon. He barely rolled out of the way.

"I think that is enough for now." Elam's voice broke into the battle, halting both combatants. "Very impressive Aleisha, I had expected that I would have to instruct you to use your magic as you did, but you don't seem to need much help at all. Perhaps the effect of being the daughter of one of the greatest Darksouls of our time."

"I never told you he was my father." Aleisha glared at the old man when he dared to mention Tallen.

"No, I did." Syris smirked at her, winking before he continued. "I used to visit Cedrick every year to negotiate the, um, safe transportation of some valuable cloth. I remembered meeting you there. Cedrick did so love bragging about his favorite slave."

"Who else have you told?" she growled at the arrogant fool in front of her.

"No one, I assure you. I only thought it important for Elam to know which Darksoul he had found. I remembered hearing him mumble about some Dictator being offered a child by Tallen, he supposedly refused, but never appeared to replace the babe." Aleisha shook as she glared at him, "I couldn't remember the name of the Dictator, so I told Elam, figuring that he would." He shuddered as Aleisha continued to glare at him.

"Calm yourself Aleisha, it is an honor to be the chosen babe of one of the original three. You should be proud Briganti is your Dictator, not upset that we know." The old man approached her, gently pulling her weapon from her hands before she could decide to use it on his apprentice. He then turned and walked calmly into the library, collecting Syris' swords as he passed.

Aleisha moved to follow the old man but was stopped by the threatening tone of Syris' whisper, "You should be grateful I didn't tell your precious reptiles, they would have been even more infuriated by your deception."

She spun around, sending him flying back several feet before crashing into a bale of hay that had been set up as a target. *Be angry, and do not sin.* She flinched as she remembered Conner's gentle reprimand. She turned away from the wretched man, refusing to become what her friends believed her to be.

Inside, she walked past Elam towards her room, never giving him a glance as she hurried to hide her tears.

Slamming her bedroom door behind her, she sat and leaned her back on the door, sobbing.

Byron hated Darksouls because of what Tallen did to Lorahlie; Conner and the other dragons hated them because most Darksouls were just like Tallen. They were known to be cruel and angry, often hurting those who had offended them and withholding any measure of grace from those who needed it.

She sobbed as she realized the description seemed to fit her. How many times had she lashed out in anger? She had hurt Briganti, terrified the people of Puko, strangled Finley, had just thrown Syris across the yard, and had even hurt Conner while he was trying to train her. Why had it taken them seeing her true form to figure out her true identity?

Conner liked to say that she couldn't be a Darksoul because she didn't have enough evil in her. He was wrong. She had anger. Anger, when gone unchecked, begat violence and evil. She had plenty of anger, and plenty of evil, to be a Darksoul.

Chapter 22

A soft knock woke Aleisha. She was sitting with her back propped against the door. It took her a moment to remember what she was doing there, indulging in self-hate and self-pity. She shook her head, disgusted with herself, then stood and opened the door. "I think it would be wise for you to leave as soon as possible," Elam stood outside her bedroom, looking both stern and sympathetic at the same time.

"He called them lizards!" She couldn't believe he would put this one on her, "he was looking for a fight, and I-"

"And you gave him one." He sighed deeply, shaking his head, "I've drawn up a map for you to follow to your father's castle. I think that, if you practice your swordsmanship on your way, and if you are patient enough to be sure that Tallen is not around when you act, you shouldn't have much trouble rescuing your mother." She turned and claimed a seat on her bed. "I think that it will do you good to have something important to focus on. If you stay here, if you continue to dwell on your circumstances and continue to listen to Syris' goading, you will become the very thing that you hate. If, however, you focus on rescuing your mother, you will be reminded of the fact that she wanted better for you than to be the daughter of her captor." He stepped farther into her room and placed a piece of parchment on her bed. "Come see me when you're ready to leave." He turned and left her in silence as he closed the door with a soft click.

Minutes passed without even the slightest of movements. She wasn't sure she was ready to journey alone, but then again, she wasn't sure she ever would be. Shaking her head in defeat, she stood and walked over to the desk, picking up her sack and shoving her few dresses into it. She glanced at Elam's map, noting that he had left her with detailed instructions on how to interpret it; she wondered if he knew that she had never read a map before. Folding it neatly, she slipped it into her side pocket, following it with her mother's map.

Having finished packing her few possessions, again, she lifted her sack to her shoulder and headed to the library kitchen, where she filled it the rest of the way with provisions for her journey. With her sack in one hand, and a newly filled wineskin in the other, she made her way toward Elam's study table.

"I'm ready," the old man looked up abruptly, obviously startled by her sudden appearance.

"Good, good." He nodded as he moved several papers to clear the table that separated them, "Have you looked at the map?"

She nodded, "The castle is on the other side of Might City. It'll take me a month to get there."

Elam reached beneath his chair and pulled a large bundle out from under it, "Not if you travel by horse." He placed the large object on the table in front of him and began unfolding the material that was wrapped around a great sword almost identical to the one she had used to battle Syris, "Conner left his, and I'm sure would not object to you borrowing him." He pulled the sword partly from the sheath to examine it, nodding in satisfaction, he returned it to the sheath and stood to lead her to the stalls.

"I couldn't take his horse without permission; he is already angry enough with me."

"Nonsense, the creature isn't going to get any exercise staying in my stall until Conner remembers him and comes to claim him. You will be keeping it healthy, and if Conner ever does come back for him, I'll be able to tell him where to find his sturdy friend." They exited the front doors of the building and turned toward the stables. Upon seeing them enter the stable, the horse whinnied a greeting to the pair. Elam approached confidently and leaned the sword against a support beam before retrieving a light saddle from the hook beside the only occupied stall.

"But it always follows Conner. It will go to him eventually." She watched as Elam strapped the saddle to the horse, he barely acknowledged her as he worked.

Taking her sack from her, he then attached it to the saddle. "Hand me the sword, won't you?" She lifted the sword from its resting place, handing it to the old man to add to the horse's load. "It only follows him because he tells it where he is going. Since he did not stop by the library on his way out of town, he obviously did not tell it where to go next." Once the sword was secure, he turned to Aleisha, watching her as if he expected her to mount. When she had ridden with Conner, he had not been using a saddle; this could become an interesting experience. "Leave by the north gate and follow the road; you'll arrive at Might City within two weeks. Restock there and inquire subtly about Tallen's travels." She nodded, and he took her by the shoulders, looking her in the eye as he spoke his final warning, "Do not strike until it is safe to do so. Use caution, use patience." She nodded again before pulling herself onto the horse. She sighed in relief as the animal seemed calm beneath her.

Pulling the reins as she had seen Conner do on several occasions, she attempted to lead the horse to the door. He didn't seem to understand her instructions. He turned to the right and made a complete circle before stopping abruptly and then turning the other direction and repeating the same pattern. Huffing, she tried again, this time pulling more gently on one side until they were facing the door, then urging him forward with the lightest grip of her thighs. Finally escaping the stable, she clumsily rode the animal through town toward the northern road. A small child sitting on a bench outside of her house smiled and waved at her as she rode past, "Lead him gently," she called, "you're scaring him." She nodded as she loosened her grip on the reigns and relaxed her stiff posture. The horse responded by confidently picking up his pace and moving in a steady straight line through the narrow street.

Passing several small homes and merchants, she arrived at the north gate and was greeted by a young boy manning the gate. "You leavin'?" he sounded shocked and confused by the possibility.

"Of course. Open the gate." The horse stepped uneasily beneath her, impatient to continue. The boy only gawked at her. "Open the gate." It opened noisily, startling the boy and sending him running.

Aleisha sighed and led the horse through. She really needed to learn to control her magic; it had become even harder since her transformation into her true form.

Hours passed, and she could feel her muscles burning from riding, from trying to hold herself on the horse. Pulling herself upright again, she lifted her wineskin to her lips and swallowed a few gulps of the refreshing liquid. By the position of the sun, she guessed she had only a couple more hours of daylight by which to ride. At that point, travel would become dangerous as robbers and outlaws would be stalking the road, waiting for easy prey. Rather than continue, as she guessed that she could if she were willing to use her magic to protect herself, she searched the roadside for a safe and secluded place to bed for the night.

Just as the sun began painting the sky with the colors of the sunset, she dismounted and led the horse about a half of a mile into the trees next to the road. Having secured the reins to a tree branch, she began unsaddling her mount. With that task done, she pulled a loaf of bread from her bag and the sword from its sheath. After scarfing down her small dinner, she stood and pulled the sword up in front of her. Taking a moment to connect with it, she stood and breathed onto the blade. Moments passed, and she heard leaves and twigs rustling together as she pulled them into the form of a large guard, wielding a long sword. The green guard attacked.

Several minutes passed as the two fighters sparred, giving the sun a chance to finish setting. Plunging her sword into the center of the green man's chest, Aleisha sent the forest debris flying. She stood still for a moment, panting as the debris settled back onto the ground, then took a seat next to the tree and relaxed into it. She would spend tomorrow evening practicing to control her magic, but tonight she needed her rest.

Looking about her at the various loose branches and foliage, she pulled at some of the larger pieces with her magic in order to build a shelter about her. Using her magic to fuse it together, she closed her eyes, confident that no one would see her through the night.

Chapter 23

Aleisha spent her days following the endless road and studying Elam's map. She spent her nights sparring and practicing to control her power. She would occasionally hear the stealthy movements of outlaws, but only once did she witness the attempted robbery of a traveling merchant who had been fortunate enough to have given a ride to a pilgriming magician who was able to fight them off.

Two weeks passed more slowly and yet more quickly than she ever would have imagined. The days seemed to crawl during light hours, but each night she was surprised by how many days had passed.

Finally, on day eighteen, she saw the towering walls of Might City. While Fonishia had been a beautifully crafted city, designed to welcome and comfort weary travelers with its smooth, rounded walls, Might City was built as a training ground for war. Its walls were high and thick, the edges sharp and unyielding. It was designed, not with frivolity in mind, but defense.

When she neared the south gate, she stopped by a patch of thick brambles, hiding her sword among the spines and thorns. It took but a moment with her magic to be sure that it was hidden quite thoroughly. Only a few minutes later, she had arrived. Two guards stopped her at the open gate, one standing on each side, holding a long spear at arm's length, crossing them before the gate and preventing her from entering. "Ho there. What business do you have in Might City?"

"I need provisions and a place to rest for a few days before continuing my journey north." For a moment, he didn't look like he believed her, but the second guard nodded his approval.

"You'll find an inn a few streets in, and to your left, the Maiden's Song. The lady of the inn is looking for a cleaning woman for a few days, if you don't mind working for your room." With that, they each pulled their spear back, unblocking the entrance and letting her pass.

Inside Might City, the streets were lined with small homes and welcoming inns. In this section of the city, a few children played in the dirt streets, and several chickens and a few dogs roamed free, wandering about scavenging whatever crumbs might have been dropped by the children as they had tea parties and picnics with their neighbors and family. She had entered the residential district.

Elam's map had a diagram of the basic layout of the city. The outer most portion was filled with homes and inns, once she passed the homes, she would reach the market district, which would have all the merchants and countless taverns. At the center of the City, a huge training ground and barracks housed the couple hundred warriors that called Might City home.

After riding a few minutes into the city, she spotted the sign for the Maiden's Song and stopped her horse to dismount. Wrapping the reins around the post out front, she entered the inn. "Hi," a young girl came bounding up to her, offering a welcoming smile and a large mug of hot herbal infusion. "I was gonna bring this to my mom, but you look like you need it more," she smiled as

Aleisha took the mug and thanked her, "Follow me, and I'll bring you to her to get a room." The little girl turned to lead her through a large sitting room, into a narrow hallway lined with neat little bedrooms, freshly scrubbed by the strong smell of soap. The last room in the hallway was almost twice the size of the others and housed a seating area and desk as well as the bed and small wardrobe that she had seen in the other rooms.

"Mom, we got a guest already." The girl skipped into the room gushing enthusiastically at the pillow her mother was embroidering.

"I can see that, Beth," the stout woman rose from her chair, setting the pillow on the desk before making her way across the room to shake Aleisha's hand. "My name is Sophie. Welcome." She smiled warmly as she spoke.

"Aleisha," she smiled at the kind woman, liking her immediately.

"We don't usually have guests this early in the week. Did you arrive today?" Sophie led her back through the door to the hallway as she spoke.

"Yes, the guards told me that I could find lodging here. Said you would be willing to offer a room for work."

Sophie laughed as she turned into the room nearest the front of the inn. "You came in the south gate," Aleisha nodded, "Tobias always sends me as much business as he can." She shook her head, smiling affectionately. "He's a good brother-in-law to me, and a wonderful uncle to Bethany. Since her father died, Tobias has been like a father to her."

"He must be a lovely man." She wasn't comfortable discussing family matters with a stranger and wasn't sure of the proper way to respond.

206

"That he is. Well, this is your room. Did Tobias tell you what kind of work I need tended to?"

"He mentioned the need for a maid. I have quite a bit of experience as a cleaning lady."

"Oh, perfect. I've been trying to keep up with everything myself, but I'm afraid I haven't had much success, even with Beth helping as much as she can. If you'll just gather sheets, sweep, and help serve dinner on the days we have guests, I'll give you room as long as you're here and provide a week's rations when you leave. Is that fair?"

"More than, thank you Sophie." Sophie nodded and turned to leave. Aleisha looked around her new room. Much like the other borrowed rooms she had stayed in in the past months, her temporary residence offered only the essentials, one small bed was positioned near a tiny window, a wooden desk and a matching wardrobe sat in the corner on the far side of the room. She sighed as she took in the new, yet familiar scenery. It seemed she would never have a room to call home. It was odd to look back and feel like the closest thing to home was no more than a piece of property owned by a drunken fool.

She made her way back down the stairs and asked Sophie for a place to lodge her horse. After taking the elegant beast around to the stable, she unsaddled him and wiped him down with a brush that Sophie had supplied. "Did Conner ever give you a name, boy?" As she brushed the silky hide, her equine companion whinnied and shook his head, almost as if in response to her inquiry. "Well that's too bad. I'll have to have something to call you, and 'horse' just won't work." She continued brushing while she thought. "How about

Phoebe Nabors

Soulfire? It fits your owner better, but we can't really rename him, can we?" she laughed to herself as she pictured Conner engulfed in flame. He would probably escape uncharred and simply shrug, claiming that it was one of the advantages of being a Dragonsoul.

How much better things would be if she was a Dragonsoul as Conner had so desperately wanted to believe. She wouldn't be standing here alone, brushing his horse. She could almost picture Snarf and Grizwald laughing at her for her strange name for Conner's horse. Byron would be standing by calmly, pretending not to be amused while Grezald and Dagmar ignored them, and Conner would probably be shaking and hiding his face from her before informing her that his horse didn't need a name.

She happened to glance out the window then. As she wiped a cold tear from her cheek, she realized how low the sun was; she needed to get inside to help with dinner.

Chapter 24

Aleisha rushed around the kitchen, filling bowls with stew and buttering as much bread as she could stack on her platter. The local guild had sent a lad less than an hour ago with the food they were to serve the more than two dozen guests that were waiting impatiently in the dining area. For the past few days, Sophie had cooked for the six people staying at the inn, her, her daughter, Tobias, Aleisha, the stableman, and his son, but today, merchants, travelers, and soldiers had arrived. Local law stated that only guild food could be sold to tenants, and they had been made to wait for far too long already.

Placing the last of the food onto a large tray, she hurried out of the kitchen and into the dining room. All five tables fell into expectant silence upon her arrival, as she made her way to the one nearest the kitchen door. Sophie followed behind her and made her way to the opposite end of the room; they would serve all the newcomers first, and meet in the middle table to serve the family and workers.

All six men at the table thanked her as she served them, then returned to their conversation. They seemed to be discussing the trade routes around Might City. Uninterested, she moved to the second table. Again, the men thanked her politely and began talking about the fighting that had broken out in the Waves of Might, the rolling hills to the west of Might City.

She finished serving and plopped some thick stew into her own bowl at the center table. "My tables were discussing the fighting and that dreadful Darksoul."

Sophie walked back with her to the kitchen as she spoke, Aleisha had requested that she share what she heard, telling her that she was looking for someone and wasn't sure how to go about the search.

"Mine were also discussing the fighting. I do hope it settles down quickly." Sophie nodded and headed back to the table. Aleisha went straight to the table that was loudly discussing Tallen.

He'll probably join the fighting soon," a dark-haired giant of a man spoke in a gruff voice. "You know he won't let any fighting get too close to his precious abode."

"Yeah," replied a shorter blond man, "he might be a Darksoul, but he is nice to have around when a fight breaks out."

"I bet that Warden Peter will go down there too." A third, dark-skinned man grunted, "That old man doesn't know how to keep his nose out of things." He stopped and looked up at Aleisha.

"Do you gentlemen need anything else?" she spoke in her sweetest voice, trying to sound like a helpful servant.

Every pair of eyes at the table turned to look at her. The dark-haired man that spoke first grinned and made a growling noise as he inspected her form from across the table, making her skin crawl. "All right then, I'll leave you to your dinner." She turned and headed back toward the table, hearing a chair slide across the floor behind her. She could sense a huge form coming up behind her, so she quickened her pace. She hoped she would not have to use her magic to defend herself again; it was getting quite old.

The man stopped right before catching up to her, apparently changing his mind as he turned and returned to his table. "You're a fool," Tobias stood before her, revealing what had changed the man's mind about his pursuit. "you should have told me what information you wanted, and I could have helped." She only nodded submissively and claimed her seat at the table.

"Why are you trying to hear news about the Darksoul?" Sophie looked worried and a little scared. She had to proceed cautiously.

"I heard that he takes up residence near the coast." She paused, trying to justify what she was about to say. "I'll be traveling that direction and wanted to know that he won't be around if I pass near his castle." She knew Conner would not approve of her lie, but she didn't think it safe to share the true reason for her curiosity.

"You said you'd been looking for someone," she countered.

"Yes," how would she get herself out of this mess? "My mother. I heard that she resides near the coast," at least that was partly true, "but then I heard that I would be passing the residence of a Darksoul, and I wanted to be sure I wouldn't run into him." It scared her a bit how easy it was to come up with the half-truth.

"Oh," Sophie seemed troubled, but satisfied with her answer.

"The guard will know when he has joined the fight. I'll let you know when that happens, but I ask that you don't make any further inquiries or otherwise seek information on him. He always seems to know when someone is looking for him." Tobias shoved his spoonful of stew into his mouth, effectively ending the conversation.

The next few weeks passed rather uneventfully; Aleisha enjoyed spending time with Sophie and her daughter, though she hesitated to interact with them any more than necessary, as she refused to begin to care for them. To that end, most of her free time was spent with Soulfire in the stalls. Tobias helped her work on her sword play every evening in the beginning of the week, and she spent the end of each week cleaning up after the influx of travelers. Apparently, this section of Might City enjoyed an uptick in all forms of business the second half of the week, only to calm down to nearly nothing after about three days.

"The fighting in the Waves of Might has gotten pretty bad," Tobias spoke quietly to Aleisha while Sophie stood on the front steps of the inn behind her. A messenger had arrived earlier that day to summon him to the battle, and Aleisha could see that neither female was taking the news well; this small family had already lost one man to battle and would be devastated if anything were to happen to him. "The messenger told me that the Darksoul has joined the fight, so now is the safest time for you to leave to find your mother." She nodded. Satisfied that she understood, he moved past her and embraced Sophie, whispering something to her before bending down and hugging Bethany. Unable to watch the familial exchange, she turned away and looked up at the sky.

The soft clouds moved lazily across the sky. All except one, which seemed to move in the opposite direction of the rest. Dagmar. The dragon-shaped splotch on the flawless background stopped momentarily, changed directions, and flew in sync with the sky. "Dagmar." She whispered his name as she searched the sky for signs of her other friends, she saw none and had lost track of Dagmar. *"Dagmar,"* this time she called out to his thoughts. If he heard her, he ignored her.

Listening carefully, she watched the sky for any sign of her large friend. If he had been speaking to anyone, she would have heard him. Nothing. Could she have imagined him? Surely, he wouldn't simply ignore her, and he had to know she was here.

"Aleisha," she jumped as Sophie placed her hand on her shoulder. "Are you alright? Did you hear me?"

"Oh," she just stared at her. How could she explain what she thought she just saw? "I'm sorry, I was distracted."

"Yes, the sky is beautiful today." She glanced at the clouds and smiled, "Tobias said you would be leaving today."

"Yes. I need to continue my journey north. I haven't seen my mother in years and I'm anxious to be reunited."

"If you'll be looking for a permanent residence once you find her, I would love to hire you full time." Sophie seemed sincere in her offer, and Aleisha would enjoy the job, but she couldn't imagine living in the town so close to her father's castle, especially after breaking her mother out of his dungeon.

So, she just smiled and hugged the older woman, "I'll go get my things." She'd packed that morning, hoping that Tobias' departure meant that she would also be able to leave. Grabbing her pack, she made her way to the stable and saddled Soulfire. Lifting herself onto the horse, she led him out of the stable and through the town.

She found it much easier to leave Might City than to enter, the guards only cared about her plans if they involved their fare city. She immediately made her way back to the brambles to retrieve Elam's sword, pleased to see that her hiding place had been undisturbed.

According to her map, it should take her two days to reach Tallen's castle. She followed the road to a three-way split. She panicked. She was sure the map hadn't said anything about a split this early on. Pulling Elam's map from her dress pocket, she opened it up and searched for her spot in the notes. *"Take three turns toward Banish out of Might City"*

Looking up, she read the signs, taking the one on the farthest right. She remembered hearing Conner mention Banish once before; he had said that he would never willingly go to that city. She dearly hoped she would not be passing too closely by the city. She checked the map again, breathing a sigh of relief when she located Banish, at least a hundred miles past Tallen's castle.

As the map had predicted, she reached two more splits in the road on her first day. By dusk, when she stopped, she estimated that she was about six hours away from her destination.

After being relieved of his burdens, Soulfire grazed contentedly in a patch of clover while Aleisha paced nervously nearby. By the time she finally laid down with a blanket, the sky was totally dark, and she was no more tired than she had been.

She lay awake all night with thoughts of her mother keeping her awake. What would she say when she finally got to her? Would her mother even recognize her? Where would they go once she got her out?

Morning came slowly and Aleisha still hadn't managed to rest.

She saddled her horse and climbed onto his back, gently urging him back onto the road where they had stopped the night before.

According to the map, she should come across a stone path that broke off from the main dirt road; this path would lead to Tallen's castle.

At high noon, she stopped to eat a loaf of bread Sophie had packed for her, giving Soulfire a chance to graze and herself an opportunity to rest for a few hours before she made a rescue attempt. She woke several hours later to a darkening sky. Climbing onto Soulfire, she rode silently next to the road toward her father's home.

As she rode, the familiar structure slowly came into view. The moment she was near enough to see the towering building in all its glory, she stopped, unable to continue towards the symbol that had been her undoing, the catalyst that had revealed her true form to Conner and the dragons. Choking back her tears, she urged Soulfire closer, slowly at first, as she had no desire to see her father's castle any closer.

Several hundred yards out, she dismounted Soulfire and tied his reins around a low branch. She would be foolish to enter the castle without an exit strategy and going in without her sword was entirely out of the question, so she needed to find a way in that did not include going through the front gate.

The stone walls were far too tall and thick for her to ever hope of going over or through them. The gate would be locked at nightfall and the guards would be watching for intruders, so that surely wouldn't be a good option either. Her eyes fell to the moat. She closed her eyes and focused on the water in the moat, lending her consciousness to it in order to get a better view of the castle walls. Upon connecting with the water, she nearly choked on the filth of it; the stagnant pool was as wretched as the Karr River was pure. She slowly opened her eyes, stumbling slightly at the overwhelming sensation of surrounding the castle all at once.

She willed the water to begin moving slowly around the base of the castle, searching for a soft spot in the foundation that she could exploit. She found none. She began lapping at the sides of walls, subtly looking for a space for the water to enter through. Again, she was met with impenetrable walls. Frustrated, she left the water, pacing slowly as she tried to think of a new strategy.

A rabbit scurried past Aleisha, startling her and reminding her of her first real experience with magic. She had felt so exhilarated, almost omniscient. Nothing could have startled her in that forest, for she knew every part of it, felt every part of it. She smiled. She knew what she needed to do.

Untying Soulfire, she led him farther from the castle, making a wide turn around the perimeter so as to avoid the suspicious gaze of the watchmen. As soon as she was out of sight of the towers, she reached out with her mind to connect with the ground, hoping to sense some sort of passage into the castle; any good architect would have provided an escape route in case of emergency, and she was going to use it as her way in.

At first, she felt nothing more than the insects crawling over the dead ground; it was almost as if even the animals were afraid to venture too near Tallen's home. As she walked slowly through the shadows of the trees she began to feel more activity, the wildlife becoming more prevalent as she made her way around the side of the castle. Soulfire whinnied and shook his mane, startling a rabbit, which went running at the sound. A bird in the tree above them hopped excitedly on the side of her nest, watching with great expectation as her egg began to quiver with life.

Suddenly, something felt wrong. There was a large void at the edge of her consciousness, as if the earth suddenly fell away. She searched the horizon for the hole but saw nothing suspicious. She crept forward cautiously, focusing on the void, trying to locate it more accurately. To her great excitement, as she closed in on the void, she could feel it begin to take shape, as if it had been carefully carved into the ground.

She turned to follow the tunnel as it fed deeper into the trees. Excitement and hope filled her with a renewed energy as she felt the tunnel slope gently upward, indicating the end of the tunnel nearing. When she finally reached the end of the passage, she nearly ripped the hidden door from its hinges. She couldn't believe that she was finally here. She was finally going to be able to save her mother from the monster that tormented her. She was finally going to know how to use her map. She may not have her friends anymore, but she would finally have her mother.

Chapter 25

Aleisha crawled through the dark tunnel, sensing, more than seeing, her way through the cobwebs and animal carcasses. Under normal circumstances, she was sure that she would have been horrified by the entire situation, but nothing could discourage her right now. She had dreamed her whole life about being reunited with her mother and no amount of filth could dampen her excitement.

At one point, she could hear the sound of hooves and cart wheels above her head, and she sensed several dozen people bustling about. Though she knew that the tunnel must have stretched a mile, it seemed to take no time at all to reach the abrupt end. Above her, she felt a stone slab that had been laid carefully over the hole that would grant her entrance into the castle. Stopping for only a moment to sense the presence of any who might be waiting for her, she pushed the slab aside and crawled from the hole into a dark room.

She was surrounded by crates, sacks, and the odor of sharp cheese. She had found her way into the cellar. Good. She could easily get to the dungeon from here, as long as there weren't any guards in the barracks; she was simply too tall to be any good at hiding.

Sneaking to the narrow staircase, she tried to sense any nearby presences, and, feeling only one at the far end of the barracks, she began her descent, assuming that the lone figure was sleeping. As she rounded the corner into the guards' quarters, though, she saw that she had made a terrible mistake.

The lone figure, which had appeared to be lying down, was, in fact, several guards sitting at a table, all of whom were now looking directly at her. She knew that, if she chose to run, she would likely not make a successful escape and she would be even less likely to make it back into the castle a second time to save her mother. She had to rescue her now, or she would never have another chance.

One of the guards stood from his seat at the table and began walking menacingly towards her. "What do we have here?" The repulsive way he looked at her reminded her of the sailor, Finley. She needed to control herself or she would likely kill every man in this room for that reason alone.

"Bring her over here, Tyson; let's see what you've caught." Every man at the table laughed, filling the air with alcohol-soaked breath.

"Don't dare touch me, you filthy wretch," again, they all laughed, even though she was sure that she had sounded menacing.

"Filthy? Look who's talking," the guard, Tyson, grabbed her around the arm and shoved her toward the men at the table. She had forgotten that she was covered in cobwebs.

"I'll have you know that I'm here to see my father, the great Darksoul," the captain flinched, but remained seated, "and he will not be pleased when I tell him of the way you have treated me thus far."

"You trying to fool us, wench?" Tyson pushed her again, causing her to stumble a few feet closer to the table, "Tallen ain't got no daughter."

"Captain Darek Moore," everybody paused, "you have worked for my father since before I was born, surely, you remember escorting me to my father so many years ago."

Every eye turned to the captain, who was suddenly looking very uncomfortable. Tyson finally stopped pushing her. "Tallen sold his daughter, even if you are her, that doesn't mean anything to us." They all hollered again and Tyson pushed her forward another few feet.

"He only sold me because he didn't realize at the time that I, like him, am a Darksoul." Every man but Captain Moore suddenly backed away from her, "Now, I have had to crawl through a very dirty tunnel to arrive here unnoticed so that I can surprise my father, and I would very much appreciate it if you would tell me where he is."

"You're lying," the captain stood boldly before her, but his voice betrayed a slight tremor, "Tallen would know if his own daughter was a Darksoul. Tyson, bring her here." Again, the large hands wrapped around her arms. This time, though, he did not bother with shoving her across the room; he simply lifted her in the air and carried her to the table.

"Fool!" She spat at Captain Moore a second before Tyson dropped her, gaging and clawing at his throat as he tried to fight off the invisible hands that strangled him. "You would test a Darksoul? You would defy your master's heir?" The captain cowered under her glare as she stepped closer to him, "I will be informing my father of your disrespectful welcome." It rather terrified her how easily she played the role of a cruel Darksoul.

"I beg your forgiveness, my lady," Captain Moore fell to his knees before her, "I did not know, I swear it. I beg you, release the boy." Tyson gasped for breath before coughing and choking on the air his lungs so desperately craved.

"Now," she folded her arms and cocked her head toward the captain, "where is my father?"

"Tallen won't be back for at least a few weeks," Captain Moore still sounded appropriately terrified, though he had managed to regain some small amount of dignity.

"And my mother? What of her then?"

"Dead." She felt her chest tighten in a most unfamiliar and uncomfortable fashion. Her mother couldn't be dead. He was lying. "Been dead for months."

"She drank the Elixir of Life; she is immortal." Even as she said it, she could see in his face that he was telling the truth.

"Aye, she did drink the Elixir, but she wouldn't reveal the location of the drink to your father. She died defying him."

"You mean he killed her," she whispered the truth that she could not accept.

"What's that, ma'am?" he stepped closer.

"If neither of my parents are around, then I'll just have to try again in a few weeks. Serves me right for trying to surprise him, I guess."

"We have plenty of spare rooms in the castle, ma'am, and I'm sure your father will want to see you as soon as possible upon his return."

"If I remember correctly, Captain, my father has a fierce temper, and he never approved of uninvited guests staying in his home," she held up her hand to stop him as he moved to protest, "I would prefer our first meeting to be on more pleasant terms than my incurring his wrath."

She could see that he didn't believe her, but he didn't appear eager for a fight with a Darksoul either, so she turned and headed back the way she came, hoping that they would just let her leave.

"We look forward to your quick return, madam." Somehow, he managed to sound like he was threatening her, as if he knew full well that she was lying but didn't dare challenge her for fear of her power. She could be certain that Tallen would know of her visit within the week.

She climbed back into the hidden passage that had given her such hope not an hour ago. It seemed so very dark now. The stench of the stale air nearly gagged her as she crawled, blindly, through the thick darkness. Or, was it her tears that were choking her? She couldn't be sure.

After what felt like an eternity, the suffocating darkness finally gave way to light as the tunnel sloped upward to bring her back to the open, breathable, air.

Pulling herself back onto Soulfire's back, she thought of her ever-diminishing options. She could not remain here or return to Might City, for fear of Tallen finding her. She could not continue her search for the Elixir of Life, as the only person who knew how to read the map was dead. She could not return to her friends, as she had none to turn to. She could never have a family, as the only family she'd ever had was murdered by the only relation she would never claim. Elam had made it clear that she was no longer welcome in Fonishia, as he saw no value in having her there.

The only choices that remained were either to return to the life of servitude in Cedrick's mansion, though Tallen would surely check there once he heard tale of his daughter, or to return to Puko and receive instruction from her Dictator. Perhaps it would not be so bad, being Briganti's pawn. After all, the thought of killing Tallen was not as entirely repulsive now as it had been when Conner was by her side reminding her of the Creator's expectation. Perhaps she would even enjoy becoming a Darksoul. Perhaps she could stop hurting all the time. She heard an awful choking gasp and wondered for a moment who was being so cruelly tortured, only to realize that the sound had come from her own throat.

She guided Soulfire back to the road and headed toward the forest city that she would soon call home.

Phoebe Nabors

Coming Soon
Book 2 in The Soul Power Series
Darksoul

Chapter 1

Dagmar was gone again. He had disappeared three times since they left Fonishia. In the three hundred years that he had been a part of this family, Conner had never known any of the five dragons he called his brothers to leave inexplicably. The longest any of them had been separated was two days, and that was always either him leaving the group to do business in a town that didn't welcome dragons, or all five of them leaving for a hunt. Never had one of them left without explaining themselves, especially for a week at a time.

"He'll be back Conner," Byron, his oldest friend and the largest dragon he had ever met, spoke directly to his thoughts, *"You know he's been taking this worse than the rest of us; he had just started to trust her."* He knew the truth of his friend's words but didn't understand it. They had all been traveling with a young girl, Aleisha, for several months. They had known that she had had magic, even that she had had soul power, the higher form of magic, but she had seemed so innocent that they had all assumed that she had been a Lightsoul.

Lightsouls are known to be kind and gentle, powerful but humble. Aleisha had been those things and only Dagmar had suspected the possibility that she could be a Darksoul, but even he had come to trust her eventually, and not two days later she had used enough power to transform her beautiful form into the dark and smoky image of her true identity. She had lied to all of them and Dagmar had been right.

Now, Conner paced by the fire and worried about his friend. *"Conner, Dagmar can take care of himself,"*

Snarf spoke now, the youngest dragon and formerly Aleisha's closest friend.

"I know that, Snarf." He hadn't meant to yell at the purple dragon, "But where does he go? He refuses to talk about his trips. I don't understand how you all can remain unworried."

"Conner," Byron chided him, again, *"we all worry about our brother, but we understand that he needs his space right now. He barely speaks about anything anymore; why would you expect him to share this with you?"*

As he finished speaking, the clouds broke as a huge gust of wind nearly knocked Conner to the ground. Dagmar was colored blue and white, perfectly patterned to hide in the sky as he flew gracefully among the clouds.

"Welcome back." Conner glared at the dragon as he landed. Dagmar only nodded as he settled between the twin orange dragons, Grezald and Grizwald. He obviously wasn't going to discuss his disappearance. Again.

Conner sat near the fire, stewing over the last several weeks. The great brotherhood that he had been a part of since he was a young man didn't feel complete anymore. Snarf, the joker, was too serious, Grezald and Grizwald weren't playing any pranks, Dagmar was constantly missing, and Conner was in an unceasingly foul mood. Only Byron seemed unfazed by the recent events in their lives, but Conner suspected that that was only because he had always felt the need to be father to all four of his brothers as well as Conner.

The hours seemed to crawl by with no conversation and none of the usual horse playing. Considering how depressing the silence was, Conner almost couldn't blame Dagmar for wanting to get away occasionally.

"Do you all realize how pathetic you are?" Dagmar suddenly broke the silence, drawing offended glares from all of his companions.

"Excuse me?" Conner looked up from stirring the fire to meet the gaze of the huge blue dragon.

"You're all moping around like you just lost your best friend." That stung, and he knew that it would.

"Yes, I suppose we are." Snarf growled at his older brother, *"I wonder why that would be."* The sarcastic tone of the purple dragon drew a soft chuckle from Dagmar.

"And why, may I ask, are you all pouting about it? It's sickening to see such great dragons reduced to a bunch of sniveling children because of a girl."

"She was more than just a girl, Dagmar." Conner leapt up to face him, infuriated by the dismissive nature of his comment, "She was our friend and companion. If you had bothered to get to know her at all, you would understand the significance of that."

"She couldn't have been all that great."

"You hated her," Conner shouted at the beast, "You don't get to chastise us because we didn't."

"No, I didn't hate her." He responded calmly, almost sadly, to Conner's outburst, *"but she really couldn't have been that great if you could so easily flee from her, no questions asked."*

"Dagmar," Byron broke into the argument, *"she was a Darksoul. You had been right, and we left as we should have weeks earlier."*

"What happened to burning the next Darksoul you met on the spot?" he shot a small stream of flame from nostrils as he spoke.

"One does not simply torch their friends." The red dragon responded calmly to Dagmar's taunting.

"One does not simply leave their friends in the middle of the Kotash Sea on a structure made only of water. One does not simply fly away as their friend tries to drown herself in said structure. One does not simply abandon the girl that one claims to care for."

"She lied to us." He balled his fists as his whole body shook with anger. He couldn't believe that Dagmar, that the most loyal dragon he had ever known, was turning on him. "She knew how we felt about Darksouls and she never-"

"She knew how we felt about Darksouls before she knew that she was one. I probably wouldn't have told you either." He was not backing down.

"If she had just told us, it would not have been a problem."

"Wouldn't it have been?" her only accuser had somehow become her fiercest defender. *"Wouldn't you have felt just as betrayed? After our last encounter with a Darksoul, can you honestly say that you wouldn't have had this same emotional response?"*

"I am not responding emotionally."

"You all are," he was now roaring at them. Why couldn't he see why this was so hard for them? *"Grezald and Grizwald barely speak, you and Byron are*

continually stewing, and Snarf hasn't cracked a joke since leaving Fonishia. You can't tell me you aren't responding emotionally." The huge beast stood and walked in a small circle around the group. *"You won't even acknowledge what happened. It's like you're afraid to even mention her."*

"We are not."

"You won't even say her name!" Again, he interrupted him. Conner just glared at his friend, afraid of what might come out of his mouth if he opened it again. *"You won't even say her name,"* he barely whispered his repeated accusation, his voice suddenly thick with emotion.

Conner knew he couldn't argue with him anymore. He was right, after all, she had been his only human friend in twenty-five years. Since the death of Byron's mate, none of them had really bothered with humans until Aleisha joined them. Sure, they had served and protected whenever they were needed, but hadn't developed any relationships until they rescued Aleisha from her master a few months back. Losing her had hurt worse than any of them cared to acknowledge.

So, maybe he was responding emotionally. That didn't change anything. They had made their decisions; she had lied, and they had left. Redemption was not possible.

Made in the USA
Columbia, SC
26 September 2018